Book Two of The Deception Series
Sequel to Web of Deception

Wrath

Of

I0525278

Deception

Ryan Hodge

SMP Publishing Edition

Printed in the United States of America

10 9 8 7 6 5 4 3 2 1

ISBN: 978-0692577301 (PBK)

DEDICATION

Dear Ma,

We love and miss you dearly,
You know we mean this deeply and sincerely.
We still hear you saying "be safe" and "let me know
when you touch down,"
Was just a mother's concern when your kids went out
of town.
We appreciate the never ending love you always
shared,
You didn't use material things to show us you cared.
You were and always will be synonymous with love,
Your spirit brings peace like that of a dove.
There aren't enough words known to man,
To let you understand how much you mean to us
Ann.
We love and miss you dearly,
You know we mean this deeply and sincerely.

CHAPTER 1
Eric's Perspective

What the hell am I doing? How am I really on board with this foolishness? I really don't have to be involved in a polyamorous relationship. I'm way too good of a man for this. I'm successful, handsome, and well spoken. I'm all for sacrificing for the one you love, but this is a bit much.

Talk about being stuck between a rock and a hard place. Yes, that's me. I have to admit that I love Sheena beyond what words can describe. That's the only logical explanation as to why I'm even entertaining this three-way relationship. I couldn't have predicted this situation and if someone had told me that I'd be facing this situation, I would have called the person ludicrous.

Now, I can't help but to think that I'm the

crazy one. Maybe I am and maybe I'm not. I know one thing for sure and it's that I hate losing. I can't just walk away from Sheena and let Kevin have her. I've always been told that love will make a person do some weird things and I guess my number is being called.

I'll go along with Sheena's idea of our family for now. Besides, I don't currently have any other women on my roster anyway. If I let her go now, I'll be spending a lot of nights by myself. This situation definitely beats a blank. I'll be certain to keep my eyes open for an available woman though. If Sheena can have two men, there's no reason why I can't play a little if an ideal situation presents itself.

Yeah, I'll exercise my options, but my main objective is to get Kevin out of the picture. I don't like the way he looks at me. He thinks he's the toughest guy in the world. He probably thinks I'm weak because I use my brain first and my fists last. It won't be hard to get him out of the picture because he's not so bright. I'm sure he'll slip up and then I'll capitalize on his blunder. I may even offer some assistance to help him slip up. Patience is my best ally.

So, Sheena wants to go upstairs for round two. I guess she has this evening all planned out. I'm going to go upstairs and see what she has in store for us. I don't know exactly what to expect, but neither does she. I'm going to give her the best dick she's ever received. If I'm on point enough with my love making, she may forget about Kevin tonight. We'll see how this goes.

CHAPTER 2
Sheena's Perspective

I slowly escort my two lovers upstairs to my bedroom. I want them to soak in what just happened to them and fantasize about what's going to happen next. I have my room already prepared for a tryst with both of them. I would've had them both come to my room as soon as they arrived, but I didn't want them to sense what I had in store for them. This move caught them totally off guard. Their eyes are fixated on the items placed around my room. Everything I have in here is intended to maximize our pleasure. I pour the three of us a shot of Patrón. Not that I need anything to boost my sex drive, but Patrón always puts me in a sexual zone. My experience is that when guys get a couple shots of tequila in them, they take a whole lot longer to bust a nut. I want and need them to last as long as possible, so I can further work my magic on them. I already have them on board with trying a polyamorous relationship, but I know they are still a little shaky on the idea. I have to seal the deal. I have to turn them out sexually, since I already have them locked in emotionally. I guzzle my shot of alcohol without hesitation. Unfortunately, both Kevin and Eric need a little bit of egging on.

I say, "Fellas, don't babysit the drink. Drink up! We have a lot more of the night to enjoy. I will take care of both of your needs."

They both listen to my urgings and turn up their shot glasses. I pour another round, instruct them to drink up and then motion them to sit on the bed. At this point we are all stark naked. I can only imagine how uncomfortable they must feel sitting right next to one another in their birthday suits. I take our empty shot glasses and place them on the dresser. I hope this alcohol helps them unwind. Oh well, it's time to take care of business.

I know I need to make Kevin bust a nut while he's inside of me. I don't want him to feel slighted because he only got to release from me sucking his dick. My kitty cat is far better than my mouth. I will be sure to pay closer attention to Kevin's needs during round two. I kneel down in front of Kevin and Eric as they sit on the bed. I grab Eric's dick and begin to stroke it gently. I also grab Kevin's dick and repeat the same action.

Both cocks are getting hard, but they need more attention to get them to the full erection. I extend my tongue from my mouth and slowly lick Eric's ball sack. His penis is becoming more and more erect with every lash of my tongue. He begins to rub his fingers through my hair. I want to deep throat him right now, but I know I need to be patient. Besides, he is not running this show, I am. I need to spread the love and include Kevin.

I keep stroking Eric's dick, but I stop licking his balls. I immediately take a firm grip on Kevin's partially hard dick and put it in my mouth. He lets out an "ahh" as he feels my warm mouth around his meat. I feel his dick getting bigger and bigger inside of my mouth. It's expanding like adding water to a balloon. Kevin and Eric are both fully erect and it's time for me to liberate this ocean of juices inside of me. I serviced them in round one without getting an orgasm myself, but I'm without question releasing during this round.

I tell both of them to stand up and they comply. I lie across the bed on my stomach with my face at the edge of the bed. Both of their dicks are in my face and I can't help but to wonder if I'm crazy for doing this or if I'm really just doing what I have to do to secure what I want. The liquor has control of me now. I have such a fantastic buzz and I'm really grooving.

"Kevin, it's your turn to get some of this good

pussy you love. Climb on the bed with me and hit it from the back. Eric, you stand at the end of the bed and put your rod in my mouth, so you can experience how it feels to have your dick massaged like never before," I say.

They both follow the orders I dictate to them. Kevin takes his big strong hands and grabs my derrière. He gropes my ass cheeks and then spreads them, so he can have a straight shot to my pussy. I order him to bury his face in my coochie. I don't know if it's the alcohol or pure passion driving him, but he puts his tongue in my dripping wet cunt like he hasn't had water for days and my pussy is the only thing that can quench his thirst. He is literally fucking me with his tongue.

I'm only licking the head of Eric's dick because it's all I can do right now. Kevin is distracting me. All I feel is his tongue penetrating me one moment and the next moment he's kissing my punani subtly. He begins gently licking around my clitoris and slowly moves his tongue up, down, and around. If he keeps this up, I'm going to erupt. Kevin is a pro at eating pussy. I'm in ecstasy right now.

Eric is going crazy from my head job because I'm only focusing on the edge of his penis. He's dick is extremely sensitive now and he can't control himself. Every touch of my tongue is causing him to shiver. He's trying to run away from me, but I don't let him. I grab his left butt cheek with my right hand and pull him closer to my face.

Kevin stops eating my pussy and inserts his extended dowel into me. My eyes roll back into my head as I feel his entry. Kevin stays true to form and strokes me deeply and gently. This is perfect because it allows me to continue sucking Eric off without fear of biting him.

I'm slightly choking on Eric's dick. Every few strokes of my mouth I release a gagging sound because Eric's joystick is banging my tonsils. Kevin's navigating my sweet spot gracefully like a figure skater navigating an ice skating rink. I love this feeling I have right now. I feel alive, invigorated, and in control.

I yell out, "Eat my pussy again! I wanna feel your tongue in me now!"

Without hesitation, Kevin begins his artful eating of my pool of pleasure. I'm constantly moaning while I have Eric's meat in my mouth. A great idea pops into my mind as Kevin eats me out. I stop giving Eric head and tell Kevin to grab the whipped cream out of my room refrigerator. He snatches the whipped cream out of the fridge and is about to spray it on my pussy, but I stop him before he does so.

"Kevin, put the whipped cream down my ass. I want you to eat the booty like groceries," I state.

I appreciate how they move to my every beckon and call with a sense of urgency. Kevin parts my booty cheeks like the Red Sea and sprays me up. He begins to run his tongue up and down between my booty cheeks like the opening and closing of a zipper. I can't control myself because the pleasure is too much to handle. The thought of getting my ass eaten is mind blowing. It makes getting my ass eaten feel even better.

"Stop in the center and lick there," I direct.

Kevin focuses his attention in the center as instructed. The whipped cream has him licking my booty hole like leftover cake batter in the preparation bowl. He tosses my salad like he has been doing this for decades. There is no hesitation in his tongue movements. His tongue is moving in swift and calculated circles like the blades of a helicopter. I squirm to get away, but Kevin locks me down with his strong hands and continues to fondle my ass with his tongue.

Kevin stops eating my butthole. Obviously, he doesn't want to cum from the doggie style position because he flips me over and penetrates me from the missionary position. He slow grinds me and rubs his hands gently through my hair until he releases. Now, I have to work on Eric. I'm sure he's ready to get off. I tell Eric to lie partially on the floor and partially on my ottoman. His shoulders and upper back are on the floor and the rest of his body is on the ottoman. I ride him in the "waterfall" position. The penetration I receive is at a maximum because his dick is pointing straight in the sky like the Eiffel Tower.

I slowly grind on his dick making sure my "G-Spot" rubs his dick with each stroke.

I'm exerting a tremendous amount of energy tonight. While I'm riding Eric, sweat begins to form on my forehead. The sweat eventually begins to flow down my body and between my breasts. Before long, my perspiration is splashing down on Eric. His six pack abs are catching all of my sweat. The sweat is running through the ripples in his stomach like water running through an ice tray when being filled with water. Maybe this is why it's called the "waterfall".

I moan and tremble with every movement. Eric's dick is bulging inside of me. I rub my clit slowly and fondle my nipples. He is ready to blow and so am I. I bounce up and down on his dick. Eric is now speeding up his movements and reaches up to grab my hips as he climaxes.

Eric screams as he begins to shake, "Sheena! Yeah, don't stop. Fuck! I'm cumming. Damn, it feels great!"

His chants turn me on and I orgasm on his hard dick. My body quakes and tremors unusually hard from all of the anger, worry, and frustration that I had built up. My body goes limp and I fall to the floor.

I wake up the next morning to breakfast in bed. I don't know how I got in the bed, but it doesn't really matter. I know one of my handsome men put me here. I must have done something right because both Kevin and Eric are still here. Eric has my orange juice and Kevin has my food.

"Bacon, eggs, and toast for the lady of the house," says Kevin.

"Thank you," I say with a smile.

Eric rubs my feet while I eat. We converse about how amazing the night was. They seem to be as equally pleased as I am. I know I put it down last night. They didn't know what to do. The sounds they made while we were fucking ensure that they are now hooked. They joined forces to please me and even stuck around to prepare my breakfast. I love both of them. When I conjured up this plan to hook both Kevin and Eric, I never imagined it going this perfectly.

I can't help but wonder a few things about what's going on. Am I just that appealing to these men that they can't stand the thought of losing me or are they extremely weak individuals for allowing me to manipulate them in the manner I have done? Maybe they don't care for me as much as they say. Does the fact that they are willing to share me prove that they love me or does it prove they don't? Let me stop questioning everything and live in this moment. This breakfast is delicious and so was the dick and ass eating I received last night. I finish eating and they clean up after me. They both leave around 9 a.m. I call my girls to set up our normal debrief session. I call Rachel first.

"Hey, girl! I need to have a girls' session. A

lot of things transpired last night and I have to bring you and Ilesha up to speed," I explain.

"Girl, we've been wondering when we would have a meeting. You've been a busy woman lately. For good reason I presume. I'm free all day today. Was only doing some laundry," replies Rachel.

"I was hoping you would say that. I know I've been spread pretty thin, but it was necessary. Let me hit Ilesha up to see if she's free. If so, I'll text you where we are meeting. Bye girl," I say.

I dial Ilesha's number as soon as I end the call with Rachel. She answers before the first ring is complete. She never lets me down with her sassy personality.

"Well, hello bitch! I was damn sure calling you soon if you didn't call me. You know I don't play no games. Can't trust an emotional man," Ilesha states.

I say, "You know you are so damn dramatic. You knew I would be calling; you do have my kids. Anyway, I told you and Rachel that I would handle it and I did. No need to worry. I got this."

"I know you are well prepared to handle adversity, but I still worry. Plus, I just be ready to fuck some shit up. These men out here will pounce on you if they smell a hint of weakness. I don't play that," Ilesha narrates.

"Girl, you know I know. We gotta get them before they get us. I wanna meet with you and

Rachel to put you in the know. We certainly need a face to face for this one," I say.

Ilesha says, "I'm supposed to meet with my honey today, but I can cancel if you need me to."

I reply, "Please cancel or at least push the time to meet him back a little. I really need to get this off my chest."

"Say no more. I'll let him know. He'll just have to wait on me. Shit, he doesn't have anything else better to do anyway," says Ilesha.

"Girl, you so damn crazy! Meet me at the sandwich shop we go to. Let me go. I gotta get dressed and let Rachel know where we're meeting," I say.

"Alright, I'll see you shortly. Whatever you have to share with us better be juicy. You know I don't like to delay getting fucked. You know I stay horny," explains Ilesha.

"Always hot in the damn panties," I shoot back as I hang up the phone.

I'm eager and slightly nervous to tell my girls about my sexual escapade last night. I'm eager because I have both of the men I love in my life and my sons have their fathers too. I enjoyed being the focus of their attention last night. Contrarily, I'm nervous because I took this path without advice from my girls. This was an extremely risky move and they may not support me. Hell, they may feel like I'm crazy. Shit, sometimes I think I'm crazy.

We decide to meet at the deli for our

luncheon. I arrive extremely early. I'm so early that I beat Rachel here. That's practically unheard of. I'm shocked that I'm so full of energy. After the work I put in last night, I figured I'd be exhausted, but I am pumped up. I could actually go for some more fellatio and dick riding. I know I'm a freak, but hell, we all have our desires. Rachel arrives next.

"Hello my dear," Rachel greets me.

"Hey girl," I respond.

Rachel states, "I wish I had your glow. You are lit up like a Christmas tree. Everything must be back in order with your men."

"Girl, stop. I am not glowing. Same ole me. My house is in order though," I say.

"Ooh, do tell. Details please!" Rachel demands jokingly.

"Wait for Ilesha to get here, but I can say I got some action last night and it was outta this world!" I disclose.

"From which one?" Rachel asks enthusiastically.

"I'll share. Trust me," I say.

Rachel says, "If we wait for Ilesha, we'll be here all night."

"She'll be here. Give her a minute. You know she's on her time," I reply.

A second later we hear Ilesha's voice. She is screaming at somebody as she comes through the door. I guess everything is in order if she's coming in loudly. She never lets anything go!

"Well next time, move your ass from out the damn doorway and we won't have a problem! Like I'm supposed to stand there and wait while you finish your conversation. Hell, I know you see me with my two god sons!" Ilesha yells at some customers who were blocking the door.

I stand up to let Ilesha see where we are seated. Also, hopefully if she sees me standing, it will take her focus off those customers. She will shut the deli down if we let her. The last thing I need is for her to get detained by the cops. I wave my hand at her and motion her over.

"Girl, you didn't need to wave me over. I saw your ass from the time I opened the door," says Ilesha.

I ask, "How'd you see me and I was sitting down?"

"You over here glowing like a spotlight. Your eyes all lit up. I wouldn't be surprised if one of your eyes popped outta your damn head," Ilesha jokes.

Ilesha gives Rachel a kiss on the cheek as she greets her and sits down. Rachel and I both go for the boys. I give each of them a kiss.

"I hate when people block the walkway. Inconsiderate bastards! Like they're the only people in here. Ummm, no they aren't, so get out the damn way," says Ilesha.

"Ilesha, we aren't here for that. Don't let rude individuals ruin your mood or spoil our time. We are here for Sheena, not them. Besides, these little angels don't need to be exposed to such ugly language," Rachel explains.

Leave it up to Rachel to calm any situation. She could step in the middle of a gang war and convince them to stop fighting. I love Rachel. I hope she is as understanding and reassuring as she normally is because I need her to be.

Ilesha responds, "You couldn't be more right Rachel. My bad girl, you know how I get when people challenge me. I don't play."

"It's cool. We know how you do. I don't like when people clog an entrance my damn self," I say.

Rachel chimes in, "Yeah, it's a real fire hazard."

We laugh because we aren't thinking of a fire hazard, but of course Rachel is. She's always looking out for everyone. I begin telling the girls about what happened at my house last night. Rachel's mouth gapes open wider and wider as the story progresses. She is in total shock. Ilesha is sitting forward as I continue describing my late night "sex-ca-pade". She is intrigued by every word that slips off my tongue.

"Girl, they went for that? Sheena, are you sure about this? Be careful. I can't believe they agreed to share you. You must have platinum in your panties! That's what I'm talking about. You have to be willing to do anything it takes to get what you want in life," says Ilesha.

"Of course they went for it! Let me paint a

picture for you of what they saw. Listen, I had this 5'7" body in a pair of six inch stilettos and draped in a black gown with a high slit up the leg. My long soft brown hair was freshly blown out and flowing to my shoulders. My strawberry lips were glossed up and popping. I strutted my red boned ass back and forth, so they would be in awe over my curvaceous body and then, like any pro, I took control of the situation," I recite.

"Girl, you know you are yellow like a lemon," Ilesha jokes.

"Whatever! You are just as bright!" I shoot back.

Rachel has a completely different point of view. I'm not too surprised though. The idea of sleeping with two men at different times never sat well with her anyway, so there is no surprise that me sexing Kevin and Eric simultaneously doesn't sit well with her at all.

"I can't believe you did that. I shudder at the idea of it. I just don't have the backbone to do such a thing. That's way past being a freak in my book. Hey, if you are happy, then I'm happy for you. You got your sons and your men. I don't know of anybody who could have orchestrated it the way you did. Round of applause," Rachel dictates.

"Yeah, I know it was risky, but I went for it and it worked. Besides, I was already fucking both of them regularly and hiding it. Now, I don't have to hide and I get to really make it what

I want it to be," I reply.

"I will say this. You are my idol. I see so much power in what you've done. Essentially, you have rendered them weak. Stripped them of the power," says Ilesha.

"She is really on point with this. Talk about emasculation. This is emasculation at its finest," Rachel comments.

I say, "I didn't see it that way going into it, but I guess that's what it is. I was only going for what I wanted. It was more about me and less about them."

"That's exactly how men operate. They only consider themselves. Girl, you know they are selfish dogs," voices Ilesha.

Rachel jumps back in and says, "Now tell me more about this 'waterfall' position. You glossed over it. I wanna hear more about it."

As we talk more, I explain how the "waterfall" position works. Both the girls say they will try it. We eat our sandwiches and Ilesha complains about there not being any alcohol at this sandwich shop. She's always looking for a drink or two. We converse a little more and the girls take a couple of selfies with the boys.

"Ladies, it's time for me to go. I have to meet my man. He's waiting for me. I'm gonna fuck him 'waterfall' style today. I like the idea of his dick sticking straight to the sky like the Eiffel Tower. I'm gonna blanket his tower like a condom on a dick. Hearing your story got me horny as hell!" says Ilesha.

"Girl, you know it doesn't take much. Your horniness stays on ten!" I retort.

"Sheena, you are not the one to talk. You have Ilesha beat these days," cracks Rachel.

"Touché. Can't argue that," I concede.

"Bye bitches. Call you soon," says Ilesha.

Ilesha leaves. Rachel and I stay a little longer and then we leave too. Rachel says she can't wait to try the "waterfall" position as well. I ensure her that she is going to love it. I can't wait to let Kevin penetrate my walls in the "waterfall" position. Hell, his dick is in my ribs when we have regular sex, so I know the "waterfall" will have him penetrate even further. I don't know if he can go any deeper, but I'm willing to find out.

Me and the boys go home and chill. My bundles of joy are asleep and I do some work. Life is good. No, life is great! My kids, my girls, and my men. I'm definitely winning!

CHAPTER 3
Ilesha's Perspective

I am a firm believer in living your own life. It's imperative that you live your life on your own terms. I am completely autonomous. I live the way I want to live and that's it. In all my years of living, I have never been jealous of anyone or wanted to be anyone other than Ilesha. I am fierce and unshaken in any and everything I do. Bottom line, if I want it, I take it. I am all that, the bag of chips, and the dip to go with it!

Now, I'm happy for Sheena. I don't want anyone to think I'm hating on her one bit, because I'm not. She is going way too far with this little stunt she's pulling with Kevin and Eric. I don't care who she fucks or who eats her ass, but she isn't even being herself and that's my problem. She is trying to be me. I am the one who makes men go crazy over my pussy, ass, and mouth. This face of mine undoubtedly needs to be on the cover of magazines.

She is way out of her league. I really don't want her to get hurt. The game she's playing could leave her hurt physically and emotionally. She is not built for the same things as me. I am the one who can fuck two men simultaneously and just brush it off like it's nothing. Sheena's mistake is that she gets caught up in her feelings. If you're going to do something like this, you have to leave your feelings at home.

She has these two fine ass men tripping over her. Yeah, she's pretty as hell, but she definitely isn't as pretty as me. Shit, my ass is fatter, my titties are perkier, and I know my pussy is better than hers. She keeps parading in front of us how good Kevin's and Eric's dicks are. I know if I really wanted to take one of them from her, it would be no problem.

Hmmm, Kevin's dick is in her ribs. I am sure my sweet pussy would swallow his dick up. My man's dick isn't even touching my stomach, much less my ribs. Kevin would go crazy over my goods. Neither of her men would know what hit them. My sexual prowess is well documented among the men who have tasted me.

But anyway, this is about Sheena and me not wanting her to get hurt. I just know how it is to fall for two men and it could be problematic if the situation isn't handled just right.

CHAPTER 4
Sheena's Perspective

I am months into my unconventional relationship and I have to say this is freaking amazing. The guys are over here pretty much every day. They take great care of me and more importantly they are stellar fathers. They are considerate of my time and space and are even considerate towards each other. I love the situation that I am in. I get to live out my wildest fantasies whenever I desire. If I want one on one action, I get it. Whenever I'm in a real freaky and kinky mood, I organize a threesome. If I want to be fucked aggressively, I have Eric and when I want to be penetrated deeply and slowly, I have Kevin. Additionally, I don't have to spend much money because Kevin and Eric provide for me and the boys financially. I never knew that being deceitful could be so beneficial. I'm sure it doesn't work out this well for everybody, but I'm only concerned about my good fortune.

We have a family trip planned to Aruba next month. I'm looking forward to that. There's absolutely no drama with my relationships. I have the fellas in check and they stick to the script. I also know my role. I am the glue that keeps everything together. I am the oil that keeps the engine flowing smoothly. I buy the guys gifts, cook dinner, and communicate with them regularly to ease their minds. Although Kevin and Eric know about each other, I still want them to feel special. I go on dates with each of them on a regular basis. I've attended a couple of school functions with Eric and several business socials with Kevin. I know this is a very sensitive situation and I have to tread with care. I even inform them when I'm going to spend time with the other one. I can't afford any missteps to send either of them over the deep end.

Tonight, me and the girls are having drinks at In the Mix. The guys came by earlier and have taken their respective sons for the night. I am free as a bird to let my hair down with my sisters. We haven't had a night out in quite some time, so we are all extra excited about tonight. I think I'm the most excited. I haven't been able to drink any alcohol in a while, since I was breastfeeding. We pull up to the restaurant, give the keys to the valet attendant, and walk into the lounge.

"Hello, we have a reservation for Mills. Party

of three," I say to the hostess.

The hostess responds, "Follow me and thank you for coming."

We are seated and our waiter comes to our table to take our orders. The service is impeccable and we don't wait very long to receive our drinks. The place is jammed packed, so we are all a little surprised that our order gets filled so quickly.

"You must be feeling yourself something serious, girl," Ilesha utters.

"Yeah, your confidence must be very high," states Rachel.

"Girls, I'm lost. You need to fill me in on what's going on," I say.

Ilesha states, "You chose to come to In the Mix out of all the places in D.C. We could have gone to twenty other places, but you chose here. This is bold of you."

"Yes, considering the heartache you suffered from dealing with Sage, we figured you wouldn't want to come here anymore. You voluntarily coming here shows that you are totally over him. I am so proud of you," narrates Rachel.

"I guess with all that dick you getting at the house, you have really put the 'Sage' era behind you," replies Ilesha.

Sage hasn't crossed my mind at all. I've been taking care of my boys and my men, so my dealings with Sage were forgotten about. I am so happy with myself and my situation that Sage and his bullshit are irrelevant. I have turned a corner in my life. Besides, it's a waste of time to worry about trifling ass men. I only have time to focus on things and people who will serve as a benefit to me, not a detriment. Sage is an absolute detriment.

"I'm gonna say it like Ilesha used to say it back in the day. Fuck Sage!" I vocalize.

Ilesha says as we all toast, "That's right. Fuck Sage!"

Rachel begins to blush from all the swearing we are doing. She wants us to pray for Sage. According to Rachel, anyone as horny as Sage needs help. She might be right. Sage might *really* be a sex addict. Rachel wants tonight to be about positivity and friendship. I don't blame her. That's how our outings should be. We don't need to bash men and make them look bad. They do a good enough job of making themselves look bad. Most of these men out here are watered down like a drink after the ice melts in it.

Rachel says, "Come to think of it, Sage is probably the reason why our service is so expeditious. I'm sure he looks at the reservations that come in. I mean this is his establishment, so you know he knows what's going on."

"Sheena, she's probably right. He wants to fuck and figures this is the best way to get back in good graces with you. We should be eating and drinking for free tonight," reports Ilesha.

"Hell, if that's why we are getting prompt service, I'll take it. I hope he doesn't think because of some service he'll be getting some of this. My pussy is well served. I don't need Sage, but hell, I will see if we don't have to pay. We can use him for something," I say.

The waiter makes his way back over to us and I tell him to send Sage over to our table. The server is paranoid that he has done something wrong, but we assure him that our service is splendid. We simply inform him that we know Sage and want to speak with him. Moments later, we see Sage appear from his back office. He walks over to our table.

"I see the divas of D.C. are in the building. You ladies are the envy of all the women in this establishment tonight. I am beyond happy you decided to join us," states Sage.

"Thanks for having us," replies Rachel.

"Damn right! We know we are the shit in here tonight. We are the shit everywhere we go! You recognize," Ilesha states. "We make your lounge look better. You should be paying us."

I greet Sage as I stand up to give him a hug. Ilesha looks at me with a crazy look because she doesn't want me hugging him. I don't mind embracing him because it's no big deal. I'm fine where I'm at, so no need to hold a grudge. Sage has no power over me and I wish him well in all he does, so long as his endeavors don't conflict with mine. If it were up to Ilesha, I would cut his balls off. She holds a grudge forever. Once a person is on her bad side, that person is there forever. I remember when we were in the eighth grade she had a fight with a girl who accidentally slapped her with a jump rope. Ilesha still to this day speaks ill will on that girl. Rachel and I always pick at her about it because it was so long ago and it was only a slap in the face with a jump rope while she was jumping. The poor girl didn't even mean to do it. It doesn't matter to her. She won't let it go and she gave that girl such a beat down that I'm sure she hasn't forgotten it either.

"Ilesha is right. I'm sure the fellas in here are spending more money because you three are in here. As a show of gratitude, your meals and drinks are on the house," says Sage.

"Well, thanks Sage. That's very nice of you, but you don't have to," I shoot back.

"I wouldn't think of having you pay for anything here. Your money is no good in my place," Sage dictates. "I hope you ladies are coming to the Halloween party next week."

"Well, in that case call the waiter back over here. I'm getting the lobster. Shit, not that little ass tail either. I'm ordering the whole damn lobster," states Ilesha.

Ilesha tells Sage that she and Rachel will be attending the Halloween party. She wants to get into the party for free. Ilesha even shows Sage a picture of her cat woman costume that she's planning to wear. I haven't seen Ilesha be this friendly towards Sage, since he and I first started dating. This is actually pretty comical. I tell Sage that I will be out of town and will not be attending the party. He is pretty ticked off that I won't be there. He tells us to enjoy the evening and excuses himself.

"Girl, you know you are always over the top. You can't order the lobster. That wouldn't be right. He didn't mean for us to order extra items off the menu," says Rachel.

"Rachel, he said whatever we want, so we should hold him to that. We shouldn't disrespect his hospitality," I say.

"You bitches can order or not order. I'm getting what the hell I want. Thank you very much. Besides, Sage really owes us anyway," replies Ilesha.

"How do you figure that?" I ask.

"I still say we shoulda fucked this place up after the way he played you. That woulda showed him. Plus, you know men only understand shit when it hits them in the wallet," Ilesha says.

We always disagree on how I handled the Sage drama, but we often differ on many things. I couldn't allow myself to resort to violence and destruction of property. I own my own business and could have gone to jail if we had vandalized his establishment. I wasn't trying to lose my livelihood over him. He's definitely not worth that.

I comment on Ilesha's statement, "You forgot

one other thing. I agree that men don't like when their pockets are hit, but they also don't like when their pride is jeopardized either. If you want to see a man broken, take his pride from him."

"Well said sister. I totally agree. That's the truth right there," Rachel concurs.

We stay at In the Mix for a few more hours. We take to the dance floor when "Wobble" comes on. This song gets us out of our seats every time. We are the center of attention when we hit the dance floor. Seems like no matter where we go, we're always the main attraction. I guess it's just in our DNA.

We are commandeering the dance floor when someone eases up behind me. I don't bother to look back because we are just dancing. It isn't going to hurt anybody. Before long, the guy spins in front of me. I should have known it would be Sage. I guess he's feeling real good about himself because I summoned him to our table earlier. He probably thinks I knew it was him behind me and didn't mind him grinding on my soft, juicy ass. I'll let him think whatever he wants. It really means nothing. I can see he's still into playing games.

"Come into the back room for a minute. I need to talk to you," Sage says while we are dancing.

I pull back for a moment and give a facial expression that says we have no need to go to the back room. I'm slightly disgusted that he thinks he can tell me to go anywhere with him. He obviously reads the disapproval on my face and rewords his statement in the form of a question. That is a little more to my liking. I let him know that I would come back to talk to him in a few minutes. I don't move when a man feels I should. I dance to my own beat. I'll make him wait.

I dance to a couple more songs and then I tell the girls that I'm going to chat with Sage for a minute in his office. I inform them that I won't be long and I'll be back shortly. Rachel is worried about me like always, but Ilesha isn't. She knows I'm well equipped to deal with Sage. It's not like he's a killer or a rapist. He's probably going to try to run his tired ass game on me. This will serve as another story to tell my girls about. I'm sure we will laugh hard over this.

I wait about fifteen minutes before I meet Sage. I see him behind the bar, but I walk straight into his office. He needs to know that I don't need him to escort me to his office. He walks in after me and closes the door. Sage offers me a drink from his exclusive collection of alcohol. I refuse the drink and I am not impressed. I've seen all of his moves. I have to say, he is certainly a charmer. I'm sure if we were to look at his family tree, Don Juan would be his twin brother.

"I don't have all night to talk. Why did you invite me back?" I ask.

"Well, I just want to say again that I'm sorry for what went awry between us. It was all my fault," Sage reports.

"We both know it was. It's old news and really no big deal at this point. We have both moved on with our lives. Let's call it water under the bridge. No need to cry over spilled milk that has been cleaned up long ago," I say.

"That's just it. I haven't moved on. No one I've been with can hold a candle to you. It's fact. All of these women are the same, but not you. You are special," Sage narrates.

"Men often don't recognize a good thing until it's gone. You would rather fuck everything in sight before you do the right thing. Well, you have to live with that regret. I sleep very well at night," I say.

Sage states, "I know. I was young and made many mistakes. We had many fun nights together. You remember your 21st birthday? We had a wild night that night."

"Yessss, that night was so unforgettable. You ate my pussy right in this same room," I say as I rub my hand down my face and across my breasts.

Sage notices my hand gesture and starts reminiscing about that night and our warm memories. He starts to approach me, but I move away from him. I sit on his desk in the exact same place where he ate my pussy on my 21st birthday.

"Your mouth was always good to me. It made me do a lot of squirming to say the least. I'm glad my eyes didn't get lodged because they were always rolling to the back of my head when you tasted my kitty cat," I say.

"I'm glad you remember how good it was to you. You can have another feel of it if you like. It's gotten even better from years ago," Sage replies.

"Is that right? Has it really gotten that much better?" I ask as I spread my legs open.

From where Sage is standing he has a perfect line of sight of my hairless pussy. He reads my body language very well. Sage walks over to where I'm sitting on his desk and reaches his hand under my skirt and between my legs. He then kneels down before me, licks my inner thigh, and begins rubbing my clit.

I say, "Stop rubbing it and put your face in it. I wanna feel your tongue inside of my pussy."

Sage immediately complies with my demand and puts his tongue inside of me. When I look down I can only see him from his neck down. His head is buried under my skirt. I can't help but think that I'm being eaten out by the Headless Horseman. I pump his face as fast and hard as I can. I know he can't breathe, but I don't give a fuck.

I can see Sage unbuckling his belt as he eats my coochie. He must want to fuck.

"You like my pussy still? It tastes good like it

used to?" I ask.

"Yeah, it does. Actually, it's even better. I love the way it tastes," Sage says.

"Good. I'm glad you like it. Do you know what that taste is?" I ask.

He eagerly asks, "No, what is it?"

"It's called ED and KD," I retort.

Sage replies, "I can't say I've heard of that fragrance before."

"Oh no. It's not a perfume. KD and ED is Kevin's dick and Eric's dick. Those are my men and they are serving my pussy every night. It's interesting to know that you like the way dick tastes," I remark.

Sage's jaw drops to the floor as he processes what I have just told him. He really thought that he was gonna fuck me. The oldest trick in the book is when a man volunteers to eat a woman's goods, so he can hit the pussy. I push him aside as I laugh at him and exit his office. Sage is extremely prideful. This embarrassment hurts him more than any physical harm. He prides himself on his sexual expertise and his guile. I beat him at his own game. The thought of him being down on his knees eating my pussy for nothing is devastating to him. It feels good to leave him on the floor with my pussy juices all over his face and his hard dick in his hand. It's a nice little payback for how he did me.

I find my girls as soon as I walk out of the office. They are still on the dance floor. I pull them by their hands and drag them to the table. They know it's urgent, since I pulled them off the dance floor.

"What the hell happened in there?" Ilesha asks.

"Sage ate my pussy is what happened, but it's all good though," I say.

"Honey, I don't know if that's all good. He is poison. I shouldn't have let you go in there," says Rachel. "Kevin and Eric won't like that."

"Kevin and Eric won't know. I wanted to leave him hanging like he did me, so I had to do it. It feels so good to have paid him back," I say.

"How did him eating you out pay him back?" Ilesha asks.

I explain to the girls how I left Sage on his knees eating my pussy. Right when his dick was rock hard I exited the room. I took control of his pride when he found out he was eating my pussy on the heels of me sexing other men. I tell them about the look he had on his face when I pushed him aside. Ilesha thinks the move was a fantastic one. She doesn't care for Sage, so anything that has him embarrassed or deficient in any way is good with her. Rachel doesn't quite agree.

Rachel says, "I see the point of what you did. It was necessary for your sanity, but it was very dangerous. You could have liked it so much that you could have had a full blown sex session with him. That would have really messed you up."

"Yeah, I know girl. Fortunately, it didn't go

that way and I got his ass back! I know one thing," I say.

"What's that girl?" asks Rachel.

"I am horny as hell after letting him taste it for those few minutes. I need some action tonight. Only bad thing is that both of the guys are tied up with the boys," I verbalize.

"I see Sage still has a magic mouth," comments Ilesha. "Got you hot and bothered."

"Like I said, that was dangerous. You escaped that situation, but you better hope Sage doesn't seek revenge. You know how he is," says Rachel.

"Rachel, I am not worried about Sage tonight, but what I am worried about is stopping my love nest from twitching. I'll just call Eric and see if he'll stop by," I say. "I need it rough and Eric is the one to give it to me the way I need it."

"That's your man! He better stop his ass by. If he needs to fuck, he calls you. Part of his job is to service you," Ilesha dictates.

"Yeah, that's a pretty reasonable request. All you're asking for is sex from your man. I'm sure he'll oblige," Rachel says.

I call Eric before I leave In the Mix because there is no need to leave if he isn't available. Thankfully, he answers my call.

"Hey babe. I hope I didn't interrupt you," I say.

"No, you didn't. I wanted to call you, but didn't want to intrude on your outing," Eric replies.

I ask, "What do you need? Is everything alright with Deric?"

Eric responds, "Everything's fine. My mom decided to come to my house to see Deric and then decided to spend the night. They're asleep and I went for a ride."

"I could go for a ride myself. If you feel like it, you should meet me at my house, so I can give you something," I say.

"What are you gonna give me?" Eric asks.

"It's something that you enjoy thoroughly. It's tight, hot, and very wet and needs to be pounded with a certain precision that only you can provide," I comment.

"If only I can provide this particular service to you, then by all means, I'll meet you at your house," Eric says.

"I may be in the shower when you get there, so just let yourself in. I can't wait to feel you inside of me," I say. "Don't make me wait too long."

I tell Eric that I will be home in less than thirty minutes. I inform him that I'm a little horny after the few drinks I've had tonight. I don't tell him about the tongue action I received from Sage. He doesn't need to know all of why I'm so titillated. I hope he comes to get straight to business. I don't want any meaningless conversation at three o'clock in the morning. I want Eric's dick hard and swift. I feel like being punished tonight. Maybe I deserve it for being so naughty with

Sage.

Eric arrives at my house while I'm still in the shower. When I exit the shower, I walk into my room and he's standing there totally naked. He's holding his thick erect dick in his hand. I can't wait to pounce on his stallion. I hold back my desire to jump on his dick immediately, instead I kiss Eric and he kisses me back as he pulls my hair back. He gently nibbles my shoulder and squeezes me firmly. I know he's only moments away from pounding my pussy with the force that my body needs. While we are standing in front of one another, my phone begins to ring. I refuse to answer it. This is not the time to answer the phone. Answering the phone would kill the mood.

Slow grinding is not what I'm looking for and I know he isn't either. He never is. He is ground and pound all the time. He always beats my pussy like I stole something from him. I stop for a moment and speak to him.

"I need hammer time tonight! I need drilling nonstop like you are drilling for oil!" I say eagerly.

Eric replies, "I'm gonna beat it up like a drummer in a band beats his drums. You won't be able to move when I finish working on your pussy."

Eric apparently is tired of talking because after he makes his statement, he picks me up and throws me on the bed. I go to suck his dick, but he doesn't want my oral performance. He is all about servicing my kitty cat. He lays me flat on my back and slightly turns my lower half on an angle and lifts one of my legs. He kneels down on the bed and enters my pussy. He inserts his dick into me slowly. He stretches my opening, but I love it. This is the sensation I have to have tonight. He is inside of me now and fucking me in the "pretzel" position.

Eric rams his dick into me back and forth forcefully. I am in a sexual amusement park from his penal penetration. I wiggle and squirm, but I can't get away. The position we are in, Eric has total control of my body. Each time he penetrates me I slide further up the bed from the force of his thrusts. I slide so far up the bed that I'm eventually pinned up against the headboard. Now I can't go anywhere. I have to take this dick like a champion now.

Eric bangs my sugar spot repeatedly, forcefully, and incessantly. He is dripping sweat all over my body. It's like he is in the shower and water is splashing off of his head. Eric is all business as he serves me. He is grunting over and over again with every hit of my pussy. I adore the way he's handling me. My neck is bent up against the headboard and it's very uncomfortable, but I don't care. We are in the moment of a great fuck session. I'm glad I don't live in an apartment because the way my headboard is banging against the wall, I'm sure someone would complain. The noise the bed is making against the wall sounds like we are trying to bust through it.

All I can do is scream. I can't hold it back anymore. I squeeze my nipples to heighten the sensation. My hair is a mess and covers my face. I am about to cum. I feel the pressure building inside of me. I need Eric to keep hitting that spot.

"Right there! Don't stop!" I exclaim.

Eric does as I tell him to do. He doesn't stop. He doesn't speed up or slow down. He keeps pounding me as he was all while he rubs my clit. I release a gush of fluid as a result of his expert fucking. My body is lifeless now. I couldn't even run from the dick now if I wanted to. I am putty in Eric's hands. My body is for him to do whatever he wants to do with it.

The pounding from Eric gets harder. I didn't think he had another gear to shift to, but clearly I was wrong. My body enjoys every second of him. He is about to cum.

"Cum on my tits. I want your juices all over my boobs," I say.

To my delight, Eric busts a huge load all over my breasts and falls over on the bed into a deep sleep. I am not surprised that he fell asleep. My good loving has that effect on men. It saps all of their energy from them. I get up and go clean myself off. Next, I get Eric's wash cloth and clean his dick as he sleeps. I put the wash cloth back into the bathroom and get into the bed too.

I am so glad that I got the fuck that I was looking for! I will surely sleep like a baby tonight.

CHAPTER 5
Kevin's Perspective

I can't believe I forgot to put Devin's favorite blanket in his bag. I already changed his diaper, so I know he's not crying because he needs to be changed. He's definitely not hungry. Man, I should have slowed down when I was leaving Sheena's place and made sure I had everything. Damn, I have to go back to Sheena's to get his blanket. Shit, what a waste of time. He's already been up most of the night and will be up the rest of the night without it.

I'll just call Sheena real quick and tell her I have to come scoop Devin's blanket. She'll agree that it's better for me to come grab the blanket than for Devin to be up crying all night. I really dropped the ball on this one. This is a total waste of time, but it has to be done. Don't worry lil man, daddy will take care of you. I'm calling your mommy now.

Damn, she isn't answering the phone. She's probably still out with her girls. I have no choice other than to go to her house to pick up the blanket. She can't possibly mind me stopping by to grab something for our son. The whole point of her giving me a key is for times such as this. Sheena won't even know that I've been by the house.

I'm immediately confused as I pull up to the house. Eric's car is in the driveway, but he isn't supposed to be here. Maybe he forgot something for Deric like I did for Devin. We'll see about that momentarily. I grab my son out of his car seat and let myself in the house.

To my dismay, it becomes apparent that Eric is not here for the same reason as me. He and Sheena are having a fuck session. I climb the stairs and all I hear is the bedframe banging up against the wall like the inside of the room is a construction zone. These two played this very well. They wanted some alone time, so they created a ruse to get me away for the night.

Sheena shouts, "This pussy is yours! I love this dick."

I know she isn't feeling his dick more than mine. Mine is way bigger than his. This is some bullshit. It's bad enough that I put up with sharing my lady, but now I have to worry about them having sex behind my back. Rage is filling inside me right now. I know if a doctor would check the temperature of my blood, it would be a thousand degrees easily. I'm gonna just whoop Eric's ass and be done with it. Fuck it! Every time I hear that bed hit the wall it's like I'm being infused with anger. His ass is grass.

Just as I go to open the door, I hear Devin begin to cry. I got so angry that I forgot about the blanket. I run into the next bedroom and grab Devin's blanket. I head downstairs and wrap Devin in his blanket. I'm gonna leave now to go get my son straight, but this isn't over. Payback is a bitch.

CHAPTER 6
Sheena's Perspective

Last night was simply amazing. I can't stop smiling or thinking about the way Eric manhandled me. I wonder if people can see the grin of naughtiness that I'm bearing. Eric left early this morning, so he could be home when Deric woke up. Eric is a wonderful father and wouldn't dream of putting his responsibilities off on his mother. I have a bunch of things to do before me and the boys head out of town. I'll at least throw the laundry on before I pick the boys up from their fathers. Hell, now that I think about it, I should just do all of my running before I get them. I can have this place spotless in no time without them here.

I know my family in Jersey will be elated to see me and the boys. It's been a few months since we've been to see them. I can't think of a better time to go. My business is flourishing and all is under control with my men, so it's a perfect time to go. I'll only stay for a few days. I'm sure a long weekend will suffice. I should be able to visit everybody in Linden during that time.

Okay, the laundry's on and the house is clean. Time to hit the streets. I drive to the grocery store to get some things for the boys and myself for the road trip. Next, I drive to Kevin's house. I pull up to the house and go inside.

"Hey, handsome," I say to greet Kevin.

He doesn't greet me as warmly as he normally does. He seems to be a bit standoffish. I really don't feel like any negativity right now, but he is my man and indulging him comes with the territory. Besides, there is nothing he can say to diminish my glow right now. If it gets too bad in here, I'll just find solace in how good Eric fucked me last night.

I ask, "Honey, what's wrong? Is it stress from work?"

"No, work is fine. Just had a long night. Devin was up late, so you know how my night went. He needed to be changed then got hungry then needed to be changed again," Kevin narrates.

"Oh, okay. I've been there many nights. I can tell your face is a lil tight. I didn't know if it was stress or if you need to bust a nut to loosen it up," I reply jokingly.

"No, no. Not stress and I'm good on the sex.

Just need to get a few hours of sleep. That's all," Kevin states.

I can't even lie, I really don't feel like servicing him, but I would have. I'm tapped out from last night, but I signed up for double duty, so I would've given him some. I would've sucked him off to the point where he was about to cum, then I would have saddled his dick for two or three minutes and made him explode. I don't have all that energy for another full blown sexual encounter. Oh well, he turned it down, so I don't have to bother with it anyway.

I grab my son and his belongings and make my way to the door. Unfortunately, Kevin has a sour look on his face.

"You just got here and you're leaving already. I thought you would stay for a little while," Kevin says.

"Well, I still have to pick Deric up and Eric has some things to do. I don't want him waiting on me all day. Plus, you said you needed some sleep and didn't want any pussy, so it just seemed like I should roll," I explain.

"Oh, so you leaving so you can get to Eric?" Kevin asks.

I don't know why he's acting so childish today. This is so unlike him. I really don't have the time to investigate the reason why he's being so sensitive. Maybe he really needs some sleep and is just irritable right now.

I reply amicably, "Baby, I do have to see Eric

in order to pick up Deric. I'm solely going to pick him up and then I'm leaving. This is not an attempt to slight you. I hope you understand."

We chat a few more minutes and then me and Devin leave. People seem to think only women are sensitive, but boy are they wrong. Men are some extremely sensitive creatures. I wish my visit with Kevin would have been friendlier. I'll be gone for several days and I don't like the idea of our last meeting being sour. Hopefully, he'll sleep off whatever is troubling him.

I drive straight to Eric's place as soon as I leave Kevin's. Our meeting is the exact opposite of the one with Kevin. I'm not surprised though. Great sex will make for warm feelings toward the parties involved. I only stay long enough at Eric's to put Deric in the car. No need to hold myself or Eric up when we have things to do.

I call Ilesha and say, "Ilesha, I'll be there in about ten minutes. I got caught up at Kevin's house a little longer than anticipated."

"I understand, you had to fuck him too before you leave town. You know you nasty. You are getting more like me each day. You're a bad, bad bitch!" Ilesha expresses. "Admit it, you want to be me."

I reply, "Bye girl!"

I pull up at Ilesha's house. Rachel and Ilesha are on the porch chatting. When I get out the car, they both start clapping.

"Why are you clapping?" I curiously ask.

Rachel states, "You are the woman of the year and we feel a round of applause is only appropriate. You are handling things so well. You are awesome."

Ilesha states, "Yeah, girl. You are on fire. You've gotten over Sage and played him out to perfection. You are winning left and right. You have control of every facet of your life. Get it girl!"

"Thanks girls. This isn't easy to do. The boys are looking for you two, so stop all this clapping and put your hands to better use," I snap back.

Of course, I fill them in on what happened last night with Eric. They are jealous in a happy sort of way. It is crazy that I'm the freaky one in the crew now. Rachel even comments on how I have taken over the role as the super freak among us. I'm okay with the title. Ilesha donned the title for long enough. I wonder if I'll ever have a regular relationship again. I don't see it happening anytime soon, if at all.

Rachel states, "I'm so sad that you won't be in town to attend the Halloween party with us. We would have so much fun together."

"I was thinking the same thing earlier, but it's cool. We'll make up for it at another event," I state.

"Ilesha, are you still going as cat woman? And Rachel, have you decided what you're gonna wear?" I ask.

"Hell yeah, I am. That outfit almost looks like

it's painted on. You can see every curve on my tight ass body. Them dudes are gonna lose their damn minds when they see me," says Ilesha.

"Yes, darling I'm going as a corporate attorney. I have my outfit picked out already. My costume is going to be so powerful. My presence will be felt and it's quite sexy if I do say so myself," Rachel replies.

"I'm sure you'll be beautiful in your costume, but that costume is probably like something you already wear to work," I say.

Ilesha says, "I think it's more safe than sexy, honey. I'm sure you'll be cute though. Safe fits you! It's your style."

"Yeah, I love safe. Being safe is comfortable," Rachel responds.

"Either way, costume or no costume, it's gonna be a great night," I remark.

"We would have such a good time at the Halloween party if you came," says Rachel.

"Sheena, are you sure you have to go to Linden this weekend?" asks Ilesha.

"Yes, I'm sure. I already have the family waiting on me and the boys. Well, I'm sure they want to see the boys more than they want to see me, but it's cool. Besides, I can't wait for some home cooked food. My Aunt Virginia is making her famous home fries, so I'm outta here," I reply.

"I wouldn't miss your aunt's home fries either. She puts her foot in them," says Ilesha.

Rachel says, "I understand. Family is important. We will undoubtedly miss you at the party. Just don't be mad when you miss out on the drama that you know will unfold at the party. You know Halloween brings the crazy people out."

The last Halloween party we all attended was a great one! Our costumes were the best and we had a lot of fun together. There was an array of strange costumes to say the least. The most extreme of all the costumes was when a lady was walking around in her trench coat. When she was asked what she was dressed as, she dropped her coat and was naked underneath. She informed the crowd that she was wearing her birthday suit.

All of the guys in the club loved her costume, but we didn't. We like attention, but we felt she went too far to get it. All the guys were staring and gawking at her. They were excited and screaming as if they were watching a boxing match. The woman didn't get to stay in the lounge long after she dropped her coat because security immediately escorted her out. I know I will miss something exciting, but my road trip is planned and I'm not backing out of it for a party.

"Her ass just knows that I'm gonna be the hottest thing in the club and she doesn't want me to show her up," says Ilesha.

"You may be the hottest, but not the way you are thinking. You will be the hottest like the hottest in the pants," I retort.

We all burst out laughing. Ilesha doesn't mind the joke because she knows I'm right. She is always full of passion. I guess I shouldn't laugh at her too hard because I am full of passion too. Rachel can laugh because she's always conservative. Me and the girls talk a little longer.

"Alright my sisters, it's time for me to go home. I still have a few more things to tighten up before I hit the road. I'm leaving first thing in the morning," I comment.

"Have fun and be safe. Let me kiss my little bundles of joy before you go," Rachel says.

Ilesha says, "I'm taking a selfie with the boys before you go."

"Speaking of pictures, make sure you take a lot of pics at the party. I wanna see everything that happens. Make me feel like I'm there with you," I demand.

I know Ilesha will take pictures all night, but they will most likely only be of her. Rachel will only take pictures of things that are extraordinary. If I don't ask them to specifically take random pictures, they won't.

"Girl, we will and we'll certainly get pictures of the after party too. You know I'll be taking pics and posting them all night. All of social media will be in awe over my pics. Rachel, I bet that I get more likes than you," Ilesha boasts.

"The last thing I'm concerned with is getting likes on social media. The only 'likes' I need are from my man. I am fine with those. Thank you very much," says Rachel.

"Girl, you just know that you don't stand a chance against me. I am ultra-sexy," says Ilesha.

"I'll let you two battle it out. I don't have time to listen to you two going back and forth," I say.

I load the boys into the car and go home. I turn into my driveway and pull into the garage. I don't let the door down because I have to check the mailbox. I walk to the mailbox and see Sage driving past. What the hell is he doing over here? He is never on this side of town. I know he isn't stalking me. I call Sage immediately and he answers.

"Hey, what are you doing? Did I just see you drive past my house?" I ask.

"Oh yeah, I did," Sage casually responds.

"I don't see why you are even over here. There is no need for you to be by my house," I reply.

Sage says, "The last time I checked, I can drive down any street I want to. I know you think the world is yours, but you don't run shit around here."

"You know you are something else! I let you get a taste of me the other night and now you're on my block. That's no coincidence. It's over between us and you just need to accept it," I say.

By the time I finish my sentence, Sage pulls up in front of my house. I end the call and begin yelling at him. I don't get why men can't just accept when it's over. I don't want him, but he can't handle it. I guess the rejection is too much for him.

"Umm, you have no place here. You need to leave my property now. I have no problem calling the police. You know cops are killing black men by the boatload anyway. I don't have time to be playing with you!" I yell.

"If you wouldn't have called me, I never would have turned around. You know you wanted me to stop when you initially saw me. Stop playing games; I know you still want me," Sage replies. "And I'm parked in the street. This isn't your property."

"Everything is always a game with you. You always have an angle with every move you make. Your life is like a game of chess. That's why I don't trust you. I know you drove by here for a reason. I don't want to tell you again, but I will. I don't want you, your money, or your sex ever again," I explain.

"I see how it is. I guess your shit don't stink now. Miss all high and mighty. I won't cause you any more distress. The other night when I was licking your pussy made me think that there was still a spark between us, but I see it was all in my head. Accept my apology, please," Sage narrates.

"No hard feelings, but I do need to get back to the boys," I say.

Sage gets out of the car, gives me a hug and leaves. It seems like when I'm having a great day, someone will always try to spoil my mood. First, it was Kevin being all in his feelings and now it's Sage and his nonsense. Sage did me wrong and now he wants me back. That's a man for you! He didn't appreciate me when we were together, but now that I'm with somebody, here he comes. Well, I guess I should say now that I have two somebodies. Why can't men just do what they are supposed to do? Men and women would have far less conflict if they would just do the right thing.

It has been an eventful day to say the least. I'm glad I got to see the girls today. They stabilize me when my world is shaky. I'm without question hitting the mall with my cousins Ebanee and Tamara when I get to Jersey. I change and feed my boys and then relax with a glass of Moscato for the rest of the night.

I awake promptly at 6 in the morning. The car is loaded and gassed up already. I take a shower and get the boys ready. I eat a light breakfast and get on the road. I try not to eat anything heavy when I take road trips. It could be a nightmare if I eat the wrong thing. We arrive in Linden at 11:30 a.m. I text my girls and my men to let them know we made it safely.

Ilesha texts back, "It's about damn time!"

I don't text back. All I can do is laugh because she is so crazy! I also get reply texts from Kevin and Eric. Now, it's time to enjoy Jersey and the family.

CHAPTER 7
Kevin's Perspective

I have to admit that I'm glad I came to this Halloween party. I really needed to step out of the house and clear my head. I'm still a little angry after hearing Sheena getting fucked by Eric like that. I know we are all having sex as a family, but I didn't sign up for them to be having sex behind my back. The deal is that everything is supposed to be out in the open and no secrets. She claims that she doesn't want to slight me. It's too damn late for that because I already feel slighted.

Damn, is that Eric over there? It damn sure is. I didn't know he was coming out here tonight. I see him looking in my direction and he's even staring at me. He's watching my every move like he's scheming on me. I should go over there and slam him on his neck. That wouldn't take a tenth of my effort, but I'll refrain from doing so. I refuse to allow him to ruin my night. Maybe he really isn't watching me. I could just be paranoid.

One thing I know is Sheena is not the only one who looks good and has great sex. I am very handsome, articulate, and well endowed. Females in the past have gone crazy over my dick. I have to see what options are available to me. Tonight is the perfect night to do so. Halloween puts people in a real freaky mood. I like that people use Halloween as an excuse to let their hair down and do whatever they want. I'm going to have a fun night and maybe it'll even be filled with some mischief.

My cousin is the best wingman I have ever had. When we are together, we always have an excellent time. I know his next move before he makes it and he knows mine. We are like Jordan and Pippen of the club scene. I could write a book off of the escapades we've had. Tonight is the first night me and my cousin Des have been out together in quite some time.

I say, "Cuzzo, I'm glad you came out tonight. Brings back a lot of memories."

"I know bruh, but it's not my fault. You've been playing the family man lately. Not mad at that though. You have new priorities. Gotta handle your handle," says Des.

I reply, "Sometimes I feel like I'm playing myself with this relationship I'm a part of."

Des says, "You can only be playing yourself if

you're not doing what you want to do in the relationship. You need to decide that for yourself. If you have what you want, then there is no way you're playing yourself."

"That's what's up. I feel a lil bit better after hearing that from you. I guess I'll think on it," I state.

"Cool, let's not spend the night talking bout Sheena and your problems. Let's get some drinks and take this party over like we have done so many times before," says Des.

"First round's on me," I promptly reply.

We hit the bar and get our first round of drinks. I know there are many more rounds to come. We guzzle the first shots within five seconds.

"All I know is that there are a lot of dimes in the building tonight! Every time I think I've seen the baddest chick in here, I see another one who makes her look like a five," I say.

"Well, good thing for you is that you are taken, so you really don't have to worry about any of these gorgeous women in here," Des dictates.

"The good thing about my situation is that it's kinda...well, transient, so anything is possible. Shit, Sheena's outta town anyway. I'm at least single for tonight," I respond.

Des doesn't agree with what I'm saying, but he knows it's my life. He gives me a fist bump and tells me to just make sure I know what I'm doing. He cautions me on the dangers of stepping in that direction. I hear him, but I'm doing my own thing tonight. I'm open for whatever comes my way.

I'm not normally this way, but sometimes situations force me to behave unlike my usual self. If I do something too crazy, I'll just blame it on the alcohol. I think having a one night stand will make me feel like less of a sucker for allowing this situation with Eric and Sheena to transpire. I love her so much that it hurts. I love the way I feel when I'm with her, but I become so vulnerable when she's around. Well, for now I'm just going to enjoy my night.

"Bartender, another shot of Patrón for me and my cousin," I order.

We drink another shot and head to the dance floor. The liquor is in me now and I'm revved up and ready for some partying. The music is right, I'm with my best cousin, and I have a pocket full of cash. Tonight's my night for sure. Woman after woman is looking in my direction. I know they want some action, but they aren't my type. One has a little too much flab around the tummy, another one doesn't have enough ass, and another girl's titties are way too big for her body.

I know I'm being extremely picky for a one night stand, but I'm selective in all things that I do. Besides, I'm taking a big chance in stepping out tonight, so I might as well sleep with somebody who's worth it. My sex game is way too good to give it to a woman who's not visually stimulating. I hope this alcohol doesn't start talking for me and be the reason I fuck someone I normally wouldn't. I'd hate to wake up next to a gremlin.

Me and Des are garnering a lot of attention on the dance floor. Women are literally throwing themselves on us. Dozens of women are just walking up grinding and twerking all over our packages. The freaks are definitely out tonight. I haven't been twerked on this much since high school or maybe the early college years.

"Des, I'm glad we came out tonight. Man, even if I don't hit something tonight, it's been worth it. I can't lie though, after all these drinks we've had and getting twerked on, I'm horny as hell," I explain.

Des says, "Be strong, you'll make it through the night. You don't have to step out on Sheena. You'd be better off telling her how you feel. The issue can easily be resolved with proper communication."

"I wouldn't mind some improper communication with a bunch of these chicks in here tonight. Shit! Look at the crew of girls with the Baywatch costumes on. They are unbelievable! Bruh, look at the short one's ass," I say.

Des looks over at her, but doesn't get as excited as I am. Maybe it's the liquor talking to me, but I like what it's saying. My hormones are in control of my night and better judgment is defeated. Just as I am about to approach the Baywatch crew to buy them drinks, my plan is thwarted. I see Sheena's besties, Rachel and Ilesha. I assume that's Ilesha with Rachel because Rachel is never with anyone, but Ilesha and Sheena. I'll approach them to make sure that's really Ilesha behind the cat woman mask.

I ask, "What's up Rachel? How are you? Is that Ilesha under the mask?"

"Hey, Kevin. I'm well," Rachel responds.

Ilesha butts in before Rachel could finish speaking and says, "Damn right it's me. I'm the baddest chick in here. Don't act like you don't know. Nobody else in here is wearing what I'm wearing, the way I'm wearing it! All curves and no fat."

I just laugh to myself because she is so boastful. Her swag is so repulsive, but attractive at the same damn time. The truth of the matter is that she's right. She is the finest and sexiest person at In the Mix tonight. I have never really looked at her sexually before, but her ass is so juicy in that outfit that I can't help but to think of her this way. I know she's got to have some good pussy with all that ass.

"Ladies, what y'all drinking?" I ask.

Ilesha states, "Hell, we are drinking whatever you're buying."

We all walk over to the bar. I tell Sage to get them whatever they want and I'll cover the tab. I notice Sage is even sizing Ilesha up. He obviously likes what he sees and I don't blame him. Ilesha alone is garnering more looks than all the other females combined.

Ilesha states, "Shaft. You are dressed as Shaft tonight. It took me a second to figure it out, but that's it. I'm sure."

"You got it right. I am the new school Shaft. Bigger and better," I comment.

"Shaft is such a fitting name for you. I'm not surprised you chose to be him for Halloween," says Ilesha.

I ask, "Really, what makes you say that?"

"I'm just saying that because Sheena said that you are hung like a horse, so Shaft is a fitting name for you. It's appropriate as hell! If you got a big dick, you should claim it and clearly you have tonight with your costume," responds Ilesha.

I'm hyped up that Sheena is telling her friends that I have a big dick. Of course, I don't let Ilesha know that. I just play it cool and act like it's not that big of a deal to me. I would look childish if I showed too much excitement about her mentioning the size of my package.

I respond, "I'm sure it's just like all the other guys. I'm no different than anyone else. Probably smaller."

"No way in hell. I heard your dick is like the Energizer Bunny because it keeps going and going," claims Ilesha.

"Well, I guess I'm flattered. Thanks," I say.

Ilesha replies, "Don't thank me. I didn't give you that big ass log between your legs. You should thank God. That's who Sheena always thanks for you being well endowed."

Ilesha walks off and goes to their table. Sage has given them a VIP table. Our conversation is brief, but informative. I want to beat on my chest like I'm King Kong or something. I'm feeling better now than I was before. I wonder if Ilesha is intrigued by the size of my meat. She may want to test the waters for herself. I'll have to keep my eyes on that.

As good as she looks, I wouldn't mind getting some of that. She was talking kind of slick in my opinion. I can't come outright and approach her. I have to tread subtly if I'm going to do this. If she isn't interested in sexing me, it would be an embarrassment of epic proportions. Not to mention, Sheena would kill me for stepping to her friend. I hope Ilesha drops a hint about having sex with me. That would make things a whole lot easier for me.

Des and I continue with our night. He even agrees that Ilesha may want to feel my shaft. The costumes range from simple to barely dressed. Surprisingly, not even the half-naked women can hold a candle to Ilesha. About an hour later, I see Ilesha sitting at the table alone. I figure I should go talk to her now before Rachel comes back. I know she won't say anything about leaving with me tonight with Rachel in our faces. I may not get the opportunity again. I walk to the table and sit down.

"This place is packed. I'm gonna squat here for a minute and rest my feet," I say.

"I saw you and your cousin out there on the floor doing your thing. I'm surprised you lasted as long as you did without a rest," Ilesha states.

I don't know if she's throwing me a sexual joke or not, but I don't want to miss the opportunity.

I reply, "I don't have a problem with stamina. I can go all night."

"If you could go all night, you wouldn't have your ass in that chair. You'd still be on the dance floor with your cousin," Ilesha retorts.

"I'm a stallion, but I still need to rest from time to time. Plus, I haven't eaten all day. Give me that menu," I say.

"Damn, you could at least ask nicely. Don't think you run me," Ilesha responds.

"It isn't even like that. I didn't know I had to be polite with you. You aren't polite with me," I remark.

"That's true, but I just have to make sure men don't try to talk to me any type of way. I don't play like that," says Ilesha.

I look over the menu to see what I want. I'm not really hungry, but I have to order something, since I told Ilesha my reason for coming over here is because I'm starving. If I don't order, she'll know I'm up to something. She is pretty perceptive. She might know that I came over here to mingle with her. I'll just order some wings. That's simple enough. Before I say anything else, Ilesha suggests what I should order.

"Let me guess, you're ordering the ribs," Ilesha states.

"I wasn't going to, but what makes you say that?" I ask.

Ilesha replies, "I heard you have a thing for ribs. That's what Sheena said."

"I don't know why she would have told you that because I don't really eat ribs like that. I'm really more of a seafood man. I like mussels and oysters," I reply.

"Well, we are talking about two totally different things. I'm talking about the way you be all in Sheena's ribs during sex. That's why I said you like ribs. Mussels and oysters are natural aphrodisiacs, so I know you putting it down," Ilesha comments.

This is the second time tonight she has either mentioned my dick or my sexual performance. There is no way this is accidental. She wants it and she wants it badly. She's a freak just like Sheena is. I can tell. All I can see is her mouth because of the half mask she's wearing. Her mouth is one that I want to feel on my dick. She has bright white teeth and her lips are juicy. Her lip gloss is definitely popping. Damn, she is fine.

"I know women like men who handle their business in the bedroom, so I make sure I handle mine. I don't want to slack in any area of anything I do. I treat sex the same way," I say.

"I know that's right! I'm the same way in the bedroom. Hell, I aim to please and I'm always successful," Ilesha shoots back.

I'm upset because even with all of this sex talk I still haven't found the right moment to mention me and Ilesha getting busy. I have to keep the conversation going or else it may never come back.

"What's your favorite position?" I ask.

"My favorite position is any position that I can feel a man's dick deeply inside of me and will make me cum. If I can't release, there is no point to any position. It would all be a waste of my time," Ilesha states.

"Makes sense. I got to bust when I'm fucking. Not trying to have blue balls. If the pussy isn't good, I won't even cum. I'll just stop," I reply.

"I've never had that happen to me. Dudes fall in love with me when they get a taste of this. I am well versed in pleasing men. I'm just saying," Ilesha says.

I'm tired of beating around the bush. I have to put it out there. If I don't, I'll feel inadequate. How many more signs can she give me without me taking action? Now is the time!

"Is that right? So, what are you doing when you leave here?" I ask.

Unfortunately, Rachel comes back to the table as I'm asking the question. Ilesha never responds because Rachel steals her attention. I don't even know if she heard what I asked. Damn, I should have sped the conversation along faster. Rachel and Ilesha are engulfed in full-fledged girl talk. They are talking about a pair of red bottoms some chick has on. They even attempt to pull me into the conversation. I don't care about some red bottom shoes. The only red bottom I want to see is Ilesha's when she's bent over in front of me. I'll slap her voluptuous bottom until it turns red.

What's even worse is that I spent a lot of time talking to her. If I would have known this was going to happen, I would have spent my time working on someone else. Hindsight is twenty-twenty. Where's Des anyway? Might as well link back up with him and continue getting drunk. My buzz is starting to taper off and it's time to build it back up.

Unfortunately, as I stand and look around for Des, I see Eric talking to a woman and looking over at me. Why does he keep looking at me? He can't possibly think that I care who he's talking to. I have my own moves to make. I finally spot Des over by the bar. Great, because that's where I'm headed. I need some more liquid courage. I walk over to Des and he immediately wants the scoop.

"How'd you make out with cat woman?" Des asks.

I sadly reply, "Not so good. I mean she was

flirting and I can tell she wants to fuck, but I didn't get to set it up for tonight."

Des responds, "Man listen, all that time you were over there and you didn't get the confirmation. If I woulda known that, I woulda came and sat my ass down. Bruh, my legs are burning. You slacking man."

"I know. I didn't want to rush things and come off thirsty. It's not like how I would approach a normal woman. This is the best friend of the mother of my child, who I'm currently in a relationship with. You know I can't push up on her with the same strategy as normal," I explain.

"I hear your sob story. Sounds like excuses to me, but if you like it, I love it," Des responds.

"Just speaking the truth. I had to be careful," I say.

Des asks, "So, what you gonna do?"

"I'm gonna order another round of drinks," I say as I turn to the bartender and order.

I order the drinks and me and Des continue to talk while we stand at the bar. We are mingling with some of the ladies and complimenting their costumes. Sage shoots me a few words while we chat.

"I see you are doing your thing tonight. You must be the man low-key. I even saw you over there with the baddest chick in here tonight. The one with the cat woman suit on," Sage says.

"Thanks man! I'm just trying to have a good

night. Me and my cousin are just cooling and having a few drinks," I respond.

"I'm not trying to be in your business, but is cat woman your lady?" Sage inquires.

"It's cool, but no she's not my lady. I wouldn't mind a night with her though. She is fine as hell!" I respond.

"Oh, okay. I feel you on that dog! I wouldn't mind myself. She's absolutely a sexy one," Sage says.

I quickly respond, "Yeah, you ain't never lied. That's why I was over there talking to her, but I didn't even get her number. I actually used to have her number, but when I got a new phone I lost it."

"That's nothing. I got her number on this card she filled out for the raffle tonight. I'll throw you the digits if you want bruh," Sage replies.

I tell Sage that I don't want him to get Ilesha's number for me. If I get her number, it'll be from her, not from somebody else. It'll be juvenile if I get her number that way. Besides, I don't know if she even wants me to hit her up.

I reply, "Thanks, but no thanks. I'll figure something else out."

"Cool man. Well, enjoy the rest of the night. I hope it goes your way," Sage says.

I walk back to the dance floor with Des. The place is still packed, but I'm ready to go home. I've had enough for one night.

"Aight Des, think I've had my last drink for the night. I'm gonna take it to the house," I say.

Des responds, "Word. I'm gonna shut it down too. I have to get up early tomorrow, so I need to start sleeping this alcohol off ASAP."

"Cool, I had a ball even though I didn't get to hit something tonight. It was good just kicking it like we used to. We gotta get up again soon," I report.

"Don't worry about not having sex with Ilesha. That's just proof that you don't need to go down that road anyway. I had mad fun tonight too. At least we know we can still party with the best of them. You woulda thought we were celebrities or something," says Des.

I respond, "I feel you cuzzo. We undeniably turned up tonight. Maybe I didn't need to link up with Ilesha, but it sure would have been fun."

"I'm out. Be safe," says Des.

CHAPTER 8
Kevin's Perspective

I walk out a few minutes after Des leaves. I waited a few minutes longer to see if I could catch up to Ilesha, but too many guys were crowding around her. I'm not trying to be a groupie waiting in line to talk to her. I hope I never looked thirsty like that when I approached women back in the day. Those guys look like clowns. Ilesha is turning them down one by one, left and right. Des is right, me having sex with Ilesha just wasn't meant to be. She would have turned me down just as quickly as she did those guys in her face now. This was a waste of time. To the crib I go.

I really don't feel like driving home. I should just get a quick nap in the car. Man, I didn't need that last drink. I'm not drinking this heavily again. This is the last time. I'll just drive with the windows down and I should be fine.

This is undoubtedly the longest drive of my life. Each light I get stopped at seems like an hour wait. I turn the radio up as loud as can be to keep me up and I have the air conditioning on full blast. I'm without question swerving in and out of these lanes. If a cop pulls me over, I know I'm going to jail.

By the grace of God, I arrive safely at my house. I managed to turn a quick ten minute drive into twenty minutes of agony and recklessness. As luck would have it, now that I'm home, I feel a lot better than I did while driving.

I sit on the bed to peel my clothes off. Am I hearing things or is my phone really alerting me to a new text message? I grab my phone to see who it is, but the number is unfamiliar. The message reads, *Sup?* I text back and ask the person who he or she is. The response I get excites me so much that I want to do a back flip. It's cat woman! I inform her that I just got home and now I'm just relaxing. I decide not to tell her that I really want to go to sleep.

I ask her how she got my number and she replies just as how she normally would and tells me that I don't need to worry about minor details. I hope she wants to pay me a visit. What else could Ilesha want at this time of the night? It's undeniably a booty call.

Hey, what are you doing? Ilesha asks.

I text back, *Sipping on some Goose. Wyd?*

She replies, *I'm bout to leave the party.*

Damn you and Rachel closed it down, I reply.

The reply text reads, *Rachel? You only need to worry about me. I want you to open my pussy up and close me down. That's what I need you to concern yourself with.*

She's always so straightforward. I know many men who aren't as bold as she is. I'm not about to back down though. This is what I want, so win, lose or draw, I'm going for it. The most she can do is say no. The way I see it is if she didn't want me, she wouldn't be texting now.

My reply text reads, *I definitely wanna bust your ass tonight. You were looking good as hell in that tight suit.*

She replies simply, *Address?*

I shoot her my address. I guess she's on her way here. I send her another text about fifteen minutes later to see if she's still coming over, but she doesn't respond. Why would she ask for my address if she wasn't coming? I'll wait up for a few more minutes to she see if she arrives. I don't want to go to sleep and miss out on sexing her.

Ten minutes later my doorbell rings. I jump off the bed and zoom to the window.

"Hell yeah!" I say.

It's Ilesha standing on the porch with her black cat suit on. My dick gets hard instantaneously from the thought of what I'm going to do to her. That heavenly body is mine to devour. I run downstairs and get to the door in 2.5 seconds and open it. I feast my eyes on a fearless woman dressed in her all black cat suit. I like the fact that she didn't change. I want her just the way I saw her at the lounge. My dick is poking through the hole in my boxer shorts. I don't even try to hide it. She walks through the door.

"You want a drink?" I ask as I close the door behind her.

She pushes me up against the wall and takes my dick to her mouth. I'm pinned in the corner of the stairway where the door hinges are. I can't move and I don't want to. I was so excited before she got here that I already had pre-cum on the head of my dick. She puts my dick so far down her throat that I feel her tonsils. She gags on my rod and pulls it out of her mouth. She methodically strokes my slong, while she licks my balls. She lets go of my meat and allows it to drop on her face. My cock is harder than a steel beam right now. All I can do is moan and squirm.

She spits on my dick and puts it back in her mouth and repeats it again. She is giving me head like she invented it. Her lips are soft, full, and juicy. I attempt to grab her head, but she stops me. She clearly wants to be in control. She holds both of my hands back with both of hers as she continues to suck me off with no hands. She is a wizard, an expert, a tactician. No words can describe how good my dick feels in her mouth right now.

She chokes on it and looks up at me. Her eyes are reading my body movements and facial gestures. She can clearly see that I'm in ecstasy and she is the cause of it. I see a devilish grin on her face as she continues to serve me. She lets go of my hands and grabs my ass. She begins to pull my body forward as she slurps on my dick. I am in awe because she is making me fuck her mouth.

She stops giving me head and begins to walk up the stairs. I don't know where she's going and I don't think she does either, but it's obvious she is ready to fuck. As she walks up the steps, she takes off her pants. By the time she gets to the top of the steps, she only has on her leather mask and leather top. Her pants are on the stairs and her thong is hanging from my ear. She still has her leather boots on, but I plan to beat them off of her.

I tell her to turn left, so she can go into my bedroom. She enters my room and makes a beeline for the bed. I hope she lies down on her back, so I can get between her legs and give her some slow grind dick, but she doesn't. To my surprise, she climbs on the edge of the bed doggie style. I wonder if this is the mood she's in or if she doesn't want to look me in my face because she feels guilty about what we are doing.

Before I mount her, I chuckle to myself. I find it funny that I'm about to fuck a cat woman, doggie style. What an amazing night, but more so what an amazing ass she has. I spread her ass cheeks, so I can get a look at her pussy. Her coochie is the purest and most unblemished pink I have ever seen. It looks like freshly made cotton candy. There's not a strand of hair in sight.

I have no choice, but to taste her pussy from the back. I want to please her the same way she pleasured me moments ago. I lick her kitty cat slowly. My tongue licks her gently and smoothly. I hear her begin to breathe heavily and then she moans. I stop licking her sweet spot and stick my tongue inside of her over and over again. Her pussy is juicy like a ripe peach and I can't help but to lick some more. While she's bent over, she twerks on my face. I don't move my tongue while she's grinding because I don't want to ruin her groove.

She stops grinding and I take the opportunity to pounce on my prey. If it's a fuck she wants, it's a fuck she'll get. I insert my pipe into her luscious peach and begin to attack slowly. I stroke her gently as she lets out "oohs" and "ahhs". As I speed up my strokes, the moans become more frequent. Each sound she makes incites me to penetrate her walls deeper and faster. She's now screaming like she's in a horror movie and I'm the killer.

Cat woman is not purring like a cat, but instead is roaring like a lioness. She's biting the sheets and I'm full throttle pounding her from the back, while looking at her plump ass jiggle from each reentry. She runs each time she is poked from my dagger.

I say, "If you can't stand the heat, get out the kitchen."

She doesn't respond. Instead, she buries her face in the pillow and continues taking this dick. Her coochie is far better than I expected. This pussy is like no other. I pull out of her for a quick second, so I can get a better angle. I decide to take a picture of her pretty ass and pussy. I take the picture and spread her lips to see her magnificent pussy. I literally see a puddle of pussy juice inside of her.

I put my dick back inside of her without hesitation. I need to feel her soaking wet cunt on my mallet. I have no choice but to beat the brakes off of it now. While she's bent over, I grab both of her arms and pull them back behind her. She is under my control, so I put her in the "prison guard" position. She can't run from my hammer now. I insert my night stick into her as deeply as I can. I pull her arms toward me and I ram my dagger into her pussy. I let one of her arms go. I use my free hand to grab my phone and switch my camera settings to camcorder. I record a few seconds of me serving her my hard dick.

In and out. Back and forth. My meat is covered in her juices as she cums on my dip stick over and over.

She screams, "Yes daddy!"

The room is filled with grunts from me and screams from her and the aroma of sex permeates the room. I drop my phone and grab her ass with my free hand. I smack her booty and it begins to turn red. This is the red bottom I desired to see while we were at the club. Her pool of pleasure is gushing wet. It's like someone is squeezing water out of a sponge the way it sounds. Her ass is so soft that I can see my hand print when I initially release my squeeze. I don't stop beating it. The pussy is so good that I don't want to nut.

I stop slapping her ass and reach under her to play with her clit. I rub her clit and continue fucking the pussy. Now she's pushing her plump ass back on my dick and no longer wanting to run. I take both hands and grab her around her waist. She is bouncing that ass back on me and I have her gripped firmly while I incessantly thrust her. The tattoo on the small of her back reads, "Simply Delicious" and I totally agree. Each time she drops that ass back on me it hits a sensitive spot on the head of my meat. I increase my speed, while guiding where her pussy goes because I'm about to jizz all over her. She takes her hand and begins to smack and grip her own ass. What a fucking turn on!

"Fuck me! Don't play with it, Fuck it! Hit this pussy harder," she orders while continuing to smack her ass and look over her shoulder at me.

I give her every inch of dick I have. It's like we are in a boxing match. It's Ali versus Frazier. A downright slug fest.

Cat woman screams, "Fuck! I'm cumming again!"

I feel the nut in my balls rising up through my dick. Her chants about her orgasm turn me on even more. I'm nutting. I pull out of her pussy and start jerking the cum out of my dick. The nut shoots out with such force that the first gush squirts her in the face, while she's looking back at me. I shoot the next several gushes on her ass. She quickly slides off the bed onto her knees and sucks out the little bit of cum that's left. Just as quickly as she slid into my house in the cover of darkness, she is gone. I fall asleep on the bed and don't even walk her out.

I wake up the next day with an awful headache. I hope this hangover doesn't last too long. I go into the kitchen to fix me some peppermint tea. Looks like I'll be downing water and tea all day. I have to rehydrate my body. After I get my tea prepared and grab a bottle of water, I snatch my phone and head straight for the couch. I'll be spending the rest of my day chillaxing right here on the sofa watching TV.

I wonder if anybody posted pictures from the party last night. I check my phone to see what's posted. I have a new text message. Who hit me up? It's my new lover and she obviously has a lot on her mind. The message she sent is four pages long. I hope she enclosed it with a kiss.

Hey Kevin, I want to let you know that last night was amazing. Every inch of your dick and every swirl of your tongue were like air to a person suffocating or like having an orgasm that lasted an hour. My body tingled with pleasure and my pussy craved every stroke you gave me. I needed to feel your long strong dick invade my wall and quench my thirst.

I felt your dick in parts of my body that I never knew a cock could reach. I still feel your dick in my stomach. Every time you went inside of me, it felt like you were knocking on my spine. You were driving me crazy. I was stuck between running from your dick and allowing you to hammer me. It was like getting a massage when you are sore from working out. The massage feels great, but it also makes you squirm.

When you grabbed ahold of my hips and really started pounding my pussy, I thought I was gonna pass out. Each time I felt your forceful thrust, I went blind for a second. I've had a lot of fantastic dick in my days, but nothing comes close to yours. I even found myself shedding tears because I couldn't imagine how something could feel so overwhelming. I hope you enjoyed me as much as I enjoyed you.

However, I won't be having sex with you ever again. It was a great onetime thing and it doesn't need to happen again. I also hope you are not one to kiss and tell. I really don't want what we did to get out. This can be our big secret. I hope you understand. I'm glad I fucked you, but I do feel a little bit guilty about doing so. Thanks for a great night, but please don't call me or text me again. I won't be responding.

WOW! I would have never imagined that my luck could be this good. I fucked Ilesha with no strings attached. I guess she has as much to lose as I do. She doesn't want Sheena to find out either. It's not like I want a relationship with Ilesha anyway. It was just the manly instinct inside of me that made me want to smash. I accomplished my goal, so I'm good. She is definitely sitting on a gold mine though.

She would be a millionaire if she could bottle her pussy up and sell it. I hope she doesn't think I care that she won't be communicating with me again. I really don't care about her. The funny thing is that I wasn't going to contact her again anyway. I got my nut, so it's whatever. This is the perfect payback for Sheena creeping behind my back. It's all her fault. She drove me to having sex with her best friend.

CHAPTER 9
Sheena's Perspective

My trip back home to Jersey was so much fun. The family time was invaluable. I wish we could have stayed a little longer, but duty calls here in D.C. Plus, I know better than to stay away from my men for too long. I know they need to release regularly. Hell, if I don't take care of their hard dicks, somebody else will and I'm not with that. If my men cheat, it will never be because I'm not sucking and fucking.

I don't feel like unloading the car. Me, Tamara, and Ebanee went way too far on our shopping. I think we changed the definition of "shop til you drop". Kevin and Eric will be over soon to visit, so I'll just wait for them to get here. I hope whatever was bothering Kevin before I left is done and over with. I just want to relax and I'm not in the mood for arguing or any tense situations. I could go for a quickie though. I let the girls know that I'm back in town. Rachel is busy with her "BAE" and can't stop by, but Ilesha is free. She will be over here soon.

Ilesha gets to the house before Kevin and Eric arrive. She quickly bypasses me and goes to the boys' room. When she doesn't see them, she comes flying back downstairs.

"Where are my little handsome men?" Ilesha asks.

I reply, "Well, hello to you too. My mom begged me to let them stay with her for a few more days, so I left them."

"Girl, you know I miss my babies. It's been days, since I've gotten to kiss them. Next time, you clear it with me," comments Ilesha.

"I'll be sure to do so," I sarcastically state.

"How was Jersey? How's the family doing?" Ilesha asks.

I state, "I had a great time! I ate good food, hit a club in the city, and shopped. Everybody's doing real good."

"You shopped? What the hell you bought? Where's it at? Did you get some nice pieces?" Ilesha questions.

I tell her the shoes and clothes I bought are in the car. Ilesha is so interested in what I bought that she goes to the car to get the bags. I don't want her to unload the clothes by herself, so I reluctantly go with her. I show her the things that I purchased and we brainstorm what I can wear to go with certain pieces. I show her a skirt I bought and tell her what I plan to wear with it.

"Ooh girl, no! You should wear your black peep toes with that skirt. It will look a whole lot better. Trust me on this one. I know you put your outfits together, but I know best," Ilesha says.

I disagree with her. I think the closed toe stiletto will look much better and will really bring the outfit together. We go back and forth over who is right. Normally, Rachel would be in on this conversation and would set the record straight. Unfortunately, she isn't here, so we have to go to "plan B" to settle the dispute. I have to try on the outfit with the two different pairs of shoes to see who's right.

I try on the peep toe shoes with the outfit and I have to admit it looks gorgeous. After that, I try on the closed toe stiletto. There is a clear cut winner.

"Girl, you are right. The peep toe looks way better with the skirt. The closed toe makes my foot look huge with this skirt for some reason and it's not as sexy," I say.

"Bitch, I told you it would look better. You know I'm the queen of fashion in the trio. Not to take anything from you and Rachel, but I'm just telling the truth," Ilesha boasts.

She is so boastful. With everything she does, she proclaims herself to be the best at. In many instances, she is right. My girl is sharp and there is no denying that. She's sharp with her tongue and her style. We have another dispute about another outfit, so I model it. I turn towards the mirror, so I can see how my booty looks in the dress.

"Baby, that looks good on you. It's holding you in all the right places. You might have to let me wear that girl. I think my ass will look better than yours in it," says Ilesha.

"You see the way this dress is hugging my ass. I know I got you beat on this one," I reply confidently.

Ilesha starts pulling off her clothes before I barely finish my sentence. I take off the dress and hand it to her. She is stunning in the dress. My girl is beautiful, to say the least. She turns to the mirror to get a back shot, but she isn't talking trash like she initially was. I think she realizes the truth.

"Girl, I'm killing this dress. I really am, but it absolutely looks better on you," Ilesha reports.

"What about my ass versus yours?" I ask.

"Your ass is juicy as hell. Looks better than mine does in it! I see why your men are hanging on your every movement and whim," Ilesha says.

We laugh and continue to talk more fashion. I'm glad the fellas aren't here yet because it gives us time to catch up on what's been happening over the last few days. I saw all of the pictures that everybody posted on Facebook and Instagram from the Halloween and after parties.

They looked really nice and seemed like it was a great night.

"How was the party?" I ask.

Ilesha responds, "Sheena, I wasn't gonna say anything if you didn't ask, but…."

I cut her off before she finishes her sentence.

I angrily ask, "What happened?"

"I know something went down. You saw Kevin at the party flirting. Let me guess, Eric was there. See how these men do. They are always up to something. I leave town for a few days and they have to misbehave," I continue.

"Sheena, calm down. That's not what I was going to say. I was gonna say that you missed a great night!" Ilesha replies.

"Did I girl?" I ask.

Ilesha says, "Yes, you did. I think of all the parties to be at, this was the one. They had multiple DJs set up like normal. Sage did a money drop this year and had a raffle set up. He really did it big this year. Not to mention, a couple of celebrities were there. One even tried to get with me."

Ilesha tells me about how Kevin was at the party and she picked at him over his costume. She reported that her and Rachel had a fun night. She liked the fact that they didn't pay for anything because Sage covered most of their tab and Kevin picked up the rest. I really think she liked the party so much because she won a hundred dollars for having on the sexiest costume. I saw the pictures, so I'm sure every dude in there was in awe over her.

Eric walks through the door. He has a teddy bear, a flower, and a big welcome home card. You would think that I've been gone for a month. I think it's too much for me to only have been away for a few days, but it's a sweet gesture. I smile and give him a warm embrace and a kiss. I put him to work as soon as he lets me go. I tell him I need my stuff out of the car and he gets right to it.

While Eric's unloading the car, Kevin comes in. He doesn't have any gifts, but he immediately hugs and kisses me. He tells me that he is glad to see me and that he missed me. I'm glad he's like his old self and not carrying an attitude. Whatever was nagging him before I left is no longer an issue. Maybe he really was tired from not getting any sleep. Kevin greets Ilesha and she returns the greeting.

"Girl, that's my cue. I'm gonna get outta here and let you have your time. I gotta get some groceries. I have no food in the house," Ilesha reports.

Ilesha gives me a hug and leaves. She gives Kevin a half-hearted wave and leaves in a hurry. Kevin goes to my car to help Eric with my belongings. I go to the kitchen and pour a drink. Kevin brings my new trash can into the kitchen and Eric brings some grocery bags to the kitchen.

"Is that all of the stuff out of the car?" I ask.

"Yes, that's everything. I checked the back seat too and didn't see anything else. Well, I didn't see any more groceries, but I did see a lot of dirt. I'll wash the car for you soon," Eric reports.

"Thanks honey. I appreciate it," I respond.

Kevin doesn't take well to Eric's reply. It is almost like he's irritated by Eric. Kevin's sour mood could be because of Eric. I hope he isn't threatened by Eric. I don't see why he would be threatened. We are a family and our situation is working.

"Sheena didn't ask you about getting the car washed, she only asked about the groceries. My man, you are more talk than anything," Kevin comments. "Just stick to what she asks."

"What I do around here really isn't any of your damn business. You should do a better job of managing yourself and not worrying about what another grown man does," replies Eric.

Kevin shoots back, "If I notice the car is dirty, I just start washing it. I don't come tell her to get approval and kudos. You are a person who seeks kudos and I don't like that. I do a great job of managing myself; I just see you are a tad bit inept when it comes to being a man. You're kinda soft."

Eric and Kevin are standing face to face. Neither one of them is backing down or flinching. I don't know what to do. Should I mind my business or should I intervene? If I do step in between them, what will I say?

"Kinda soft? I got your kinda soft. I'll tell you right now that you don't ever want our two streets to meet!" exclaims Eric.

"All of that is tough talk. Ain't really worried about that. What I know is this, if we go to throwing blows, everybody is gonna know that you were in a fight," remarks Kevin.

All of this ominous talk has me scared. I'm happy the boys aren't here. I know it's not a good idea for me to step in between two angry men who are six feet tall. They both have their eyes locked in on the other's eyes like two Rottweilers about to fight at Michael Vick's house. With fists tightly closed and anger in their eyes, they stand before one another.

"Fellas! It's not that serious. You are two different men with two different ways of achieving the same goal. It doesn't matter. I know your sons aren't here, but you know this isn't appropriate behavior for them to see," I say.

Kevin looks over at me and I can see him weighing what I said. He chuckles and takes a few steps out of Eric's face. When he steps back a few feet, so does Eric. I let out a slight sigh of relief. That was very intense. If they fought, they certainly would have trashed my place. I'm glad I was able to diffuse the situation. I know a lot of women would be happy that they have two men ready to fight over her, but I'm not. It's actually too much drama for me. I am so far past my drama liking days.

"Guys, I think you both should leave to give yourselves some time to cool off," I say.

There is no resistance from either one of them. Eric walks out through the garage door and Kevin leaves through the front door. Maybe things will be a little better in a few days. I need all of this friction to be resolved before the boys return home.

It's my first day back in town and there's already drama. I'd rather be sitting here with my men drinking wine and laughing, but I'm not that lucky today. I guess I could look on the bright side of things. At least I can sit here and chill by myself. I don't have to worry about entertaining them. If I choose to do nothing, that's just what it is. Talk about no pressure. I'll find solace in relaxing. I didn't relax much while in Linden anyway.

As I pour my glass of wine, I hear shouting from outside. I run to the front door and see Kevin and Eric haven't left yet. Kevin is out of his car and Eric is still in his. My nerves can't take this. I thought I was out of high school. Hell, if I am, it sure doesn't seem like it.

I ask, "What's the problem now?"

"Your boy can't drive is the problem. He wants me to move my car out of his way, but he has enough room to get out. If he could handle the wheel, he could get out with no problem," Kevin narrates.

Eric states, "All you have to do is pull up a few feet and this conversation wouldn't be happening. You are a real petty dude. I should ram into your car, since you don't want to move it."

"I will move it as soon as I come out the house. I'm not getting in the car to pull up two feet and then getting back out of the car to run in the house just to run back to the car to leave. I ain't doing all that," Kevin explains.

"See, this is the bullshit that gets people hurt. Bruh, I'm not sitting here waiting for you to do shit. Move your damn car. I'm tired of playing with you!" Eric screams.

Tempers are flaring more now than in the house. I try to calm the situation again, but my efforts are futile. They aren't paying me any mind. I even attempt to get Kevin's keys, but he won't give them to me. He is intent on making Eric wait.

"If I have to wait, so does he. He gets special treatment and I'm second string. Nah, he can wait for me this time," says Kevin.

I have no idea what he's ranting about. I question if he even knows what he's talking about. He storms by me and enters the house. Eric gets out of his car and examines the space he has to back out. He probably could make it through without hitting Kevin's car, but it'll be tight. I know I wouldn't chance it. Kevin comes out of the house with an apple in his hand. I know he didn't go in the house just for an apple.

Eric sees Kevin holding the apple and becomes infuriated.

"I know you don't have me waiting for you to get an apple," says Eric. "I should slap that damn apple out your hand."

Why is Kevin being so paltry? Why is he antagonizing Eric? They were getting along just fine and now Kevin is causing problems. Something is wrong and I need to know what it is.

"See, that's the difference between a man and a boy. If you were a man, you wouldn't announce that you would knock the apple out of my hand. You'd just do it," Kevin says while he approaches Eric and takes a bite out of the apple.

Kevin confidently stands in Eric's face as he attempts to bite the apple again. Eric smacks the apple out of Kevin's hand while it's at his mouth. He doesn't just smack the apple out of his mouth; he also slaps Kevin across the face. I don't know if he smacked Kevin on purpose or inadvertently.

"Is that man enough for you boy?" asks Eric as he jumps back in a defensive stance.

Kevin's expression quickly turns from confident to rage. His eyes are open so wide that I think they're going to pop out of his skull. Kevin lunges for Eric like a football player jumping off the offensive line. Kevin grabs Eric and they both go crashing against Kevin's car. The force is so powerful that they leave a huge body print in his car.

They are locked in a rage filled scuffle. I'm screaming at the top of my lungs for them to stop, but they can't hear me. I'm stuck between calling the cops or just letting them get their fight on. What if one of them gets seriously injured? That would be terrible. Even worse, what if one of them dies? Kevin may have his gun on him. Maybe that's why he's so confident. My mind is racing all over the place. I don't know what to do.

They trip over the curb and fall to the ground. Kevin is on top of Eric as they fall, but Eric flips him at the last second and lands on top of him. Eric punches Kevin in the face twice. When Eric throws a third swing, Kevin dodges it and Eric punches the grass. Eric winces from punching the ground. Kevin uses that opportunity to punch Eric in his jaw and pushes Eric off of him. They both jump back to their feet and get in a boxing position.

Kevin swings, but Eric dodges. Eric swings and Kevin blocks it, but Kevin throws another swift blow and nails Eric right in the chin. Eric staggers back and Kevin rushes in. While he rushes in, he doesn't protect himself and Eric hits him in his stomach. Kevin bends over from the dashing blow to his midsection. Eric tries to kick Kevin in the face while he's bent over.

It's almost like Kevin baited him because as soon as Eric lifts his leg to kick him, he grabs Eric while he's off balance and slams him on his head. Eric is visibly dazed from the slam to his head. Kevin sits on Eric's chest and punches him while yelling profanities at him. Eric is defenseless at this point. I run over to them and push Kevin off of Eric. There is blood all over them.

Kevin gets up and yells at me for pushing him. Kevin is breathing heavily as he walks to his car. I check on Eric to make sure he's okay, but he shrugs me off of him. I don't know why he pulled away from me like that. I haven't done anything to him. I protected him from Kevin. I walk away from Eric to give him a minute to gather himself.

"Kevin, what is your damn problem?" I ask.

"I don't have a damn problem. He slapped me, but I'm the one with a problem. This is the typical favoritism that you've been showing him," Kevin replies.

"I can't believe you are acting like this. I treat both of you equally. Yeah, he hit you, but you instigated the entire fight. You pushed him to the point where he had to strike you," I say.

"He didn't have to hit me. He could have gotten back in his car and waited for me to leave, but he didn't want to. Seems like everything he does is just so perfect," Kevin states.

Kevin has lost all cool points with me. He was so sweet and understanding and now he's like a jealous bully. I won't deal with an envious man. I can't. I can't.

"Where is this new attitude coming from? What happened to you?" I ask.

"When people go behind your back and get freaky with other men, it tends to fuck with your head. You were supposed to be clear and upfront about things and you were not," Kevin responds.

He must be talking about when I let Sage eat me out at the club that night. Somebody must have told him I went into Sage's office. Nobody in there that night knew me, so that can't be it. Also, the blinds were closed, so no one could see inside. Sage must have spilled the beans. I'm surprised that Sage would say something because he's normally extremely discreet. Letting him eat me out was a bad move, but I needed a little payback for how he played me.

"Kevin, I have no idea what you're talking about," I say.

I'll let him tell me what it is that he knows. I don't feel the need to put it out there. For all I know, it's nothing to do with Sage.

Kevin explains, "You are fucking Eric behind my back and I'm not putting up with it anymore. I heard you screaming how your pussy is his. That shit makes me sick to my stomach."

"Are you talking about the night when you had Devin?" I ask.

Kevin explains that he was in the house the night I had sex with Eric. His feelings are hurt because he feels like we were creeping on him. I'm mad that he overheard our sexual encounter, but he isn't making any sense. He knows that I am in a relationship with him and Eric, so I don't see why this is such a big deal. He is really mad because I told Eric that my goods are his. I tell Kevin the same thing when he and I have sex when Eric isn't there. His pride must be hurt. I don't have the energy today to stroke his ego.

"It was just a fun night. It wasn't about making you feel badly. Hell, I didn't even know you were in the house. You should've joined us if you felt so strongly about it. I'm gonna need you to man up and let it go, damn," I reply.

"I'm glad you feel that way about people going behind your back. It's no big deal to you. Well, since it's no reason to get mad, I guess it won't bother you that I had sex with someone after the Halloween party," Kevin reports.

"You fucked some random chick in the streets?" I question.

Kevin replies, "Well, actually she wasn't a random chick."

"Then who the hell is she?" I inquire.

Kevin says, "She's someone who knows you. Come to think of it, she actually looks a little bit like you. Complexion and all."

"Are you serious?" I ask.

"Yeah, I fucked her and the pussy was good as fuck. Her shit makes yours look like toilet water You need to take some dick sucking lessons from her too. Yeah, she gave me head too. I know it's no big deal to you though," Kevin narrates.

I am so mad at Kevin right now. Why would he think he needed to resort to having sex with another woman? I treat him like a king sexually. He never has to go to bed with a hard on. It infuriates me even more that he is so bluntly throwing it in my face. What man would do that? He clearly means me no good.

I could stab him. She has better goods than me? There is no way her sex is better than mine. He probably scooped some young girl looking for a cheap thrill. I'm sure she doesn't know what she's doing like me. Kevin thinks he's going to break my spirit, but he is ignorant to my resolve.

"Who is this woman with the great sex Kevin? You do know that we won't be having sex anymore?" I ask out of curiosity.

"You don't need to know who she is. That's none of your business anyway, since you said we won't be fucking anymore," comments Kevin.

I say, "You're right, it doesn't matter. I hope you are happy with the decision you've made. You don't even know how big of a mistake you've made."

Kevin replies, "I haven't made any mistakes, but it really just sounds like you're a bit jealous because I had somebody with better sex than you."

"Oh no boo boo, that's so not it. That's laughable because I'm all woman. I don't have an envious bone in my body. The reality of the situation is that you're the jealous one. You clearly suffer from being insecure. Your insecurities have your emotions all out of sync," I say.

"You are crazier than I already knew. I know who I am and I'm strong in my manhood. I have no reason to be insecure. I have way too many things going for myself than to worry about other people and being jealous," Kevin explains.

I reply, "I agree with part of what you said. You have a lot of positive attributes to be proud of, but you do need to be jealous of one man and that man is Eric. You should be jealous of the way he handles me in the bedroom. The truth is that you just don't fuck me like he does," I say.

"Whatever, a hoe is a hoe. It just is what it is," Kevin states.

I spit in his face without even thinking. Kevin raises his hand up at me as if he is going to hit me. Fortunately, Eric is there and gives Kevin a push. Kevin reaches in his pocket and grabs a tissue. He wipes the spit off of his face, jumps in his car and finally pulls off. Thank you for finally leaving. I turn to Eric to talk to him.

"Eric, I'm so sorry for all of this. I really don't know what came over him. Come inside, so I can clean you up," I say.

"I'm gonna go to my house and clean myself up. I really don't want you to touch me right now. All of this is really your fault and I'm not feeling you right now. I can't go to work with my face messed up like this. What a damn mess,"

Eric remarks.

I say, "I know you are mad, but this isn't my fault. I didn't put Kevin up to any of these shenanigans. He acted solely on his own."

"This entire fiasco stems from your deceit. I didn't sign up for getting into fights and getting beat up. This is totally not my character and is not for me," Eric narrates.

"Let me do you a favor. Let's take a break from one another, so you can find yourself and clear your head. I don't want you to be in situations that you obviously can't handle," I say.

I tell Eric that it's best that he leaves my house now. I don't want to talk to him right now anyway. I can't believe he's acting like this is my fault. I have to contact the girls and let them know what's going on. They are not going to believe this any more than I do. I'm still in utter disbelief. This is a day for the ages.

CHAPTER 10
Sheena's Perspective

Kevin claims he cheated on me with someone I know, Eric and Kevin had a fist fight, and now I'm without a man. Talk about from sugar to shit. I know it's possible, but not all in the same damn day. Hell, all of this happened in the same damn hour. What's really going on here? If I would have known this, I would have stayed in Jersey a little while longer. Maybe if I had stayed, I could have at least avoided the fight between my two lovers.

Oh well, that's not an option now. Again, I have to deal with the situation that's before me. It seems like my life is one big circle. I keep having to put people in check and defend myself. Why do my relationships have to be so much work? Rachel and Ilesha never have the drama I have. Their relationships are smooth sailing for the most part.

My cousin Ann used to say all the time, "If it ain't rough, it ain't right". Talk about hitting the nail on the head. I do an excellent job of handling my romantic woes, but that doesn't mean I enjoy them. Some peace and quiet would suit me just fine. I know I won't have any quiet time for a while because I have to get to the bottom of this. I hate to bother Ilesha and Rachel with my foolishness again, but I have no choice because I need their advice during another tumultuous time. I can't allow Kevin to insult me and nothing happen to him. I call Rachel.

"Hey girl, I need you right now. Please tell me you can get free," I say.

Rachel replies, "It is apparently urgent, so yes I can get free."

"Thank you so much. It means a lot," I gratefully respond.

I tell Rachel that I will pick her up because I need her to ride with me. She's home and will be ready when I arrive. I also call Ilesha to tell her that I have a major emergency and that me and Rachel are on our way. I am so pumped up that I can't even do the speed limit. I scoop Rachel up and we zoom to Ilesha's.

I storm through Ilesha's door, throw my bag down, and head straight for the refrigerator. I am so hyped up that I didn't even speak. I need a drink or two to calm my nerves. Rachel walks in a moment after I do.

Ilesha asks, "What's wrong?"

I'm guzzling down a shot, so I don't respond. I can't even formulate the right thoughts to start the story. I'm livid from this whole encounter.

"Rachel, what's wrong with your girl? Why is she tripping like this?" Ilesha asks.

"The most I've gotten from her is that it's something with her boyfriends. I couldn't quite understand what she was saying in the car. She is beyond frustrated," Rachel says.

"Girl, you got to calm down and spit that shit out. Don't keep it in. You don't need to be angry now; you are with us. Let us help," states Ilesha.

"All hell broke loose when you left the house earlier. Eric and Kevin started arguing, but I was able to calm that down. They eventually went outside because I asked them to leave. Hell, before I knew it they were punching, kicking, and slamming each other. All I could do was scream," I report.

"Oh hell, I knew it was only a matter of time before they locked ass. Men are too prideful to share a beautiful woman like you without there being turmoil," explains Ilesha.

Rachel comments, "There is too much violence in the world. I wish they would have resolved it without putting hands on each other. I'm sure that was a nightmare. Sister, I'm so sorry. Give me a hug."

I give her a hug and it makes me feel a little

bit better. Maybe it's not the hug. It could be that the drink is starting to calm my nerves.

"I'm sure Eric got his ass beat. He just doesn't look like he can handle Kevin. Kevin seems mean and angry for some reason," says Ilesha.

"You did the right thing by not trying to get in the way of them. A woman should never step in between two grown men fighting. They could have hit you accidentally," remarks Rachel.

"And then Rachel and I would have had to whoop some ass!" Ilesha chimes in.

I inform them that I almost got hit by Kevin. They are both extremely upset when I tell them that he raised his hand to hit me. They both give praise to Eric for stopping Kevin from slapping me or even worse. With his temper, he may have beaten me down. Rachel calls Kevin a coward and of course Ilesha calls him a pussy.

"Why was Kevin about to hit you? Why would he turn his attention to you?" asks Rachel.

"Well, it's kinda my fault. I'll be honest and admit that I provoked him. I spit in his face, so I guess he should have been angry," I report.

"Damn, I can't believe he didn't throw you into the side of the house. I would have gone for blood if someone spit on me," Ilesha says. "I don't play that. But it's lucky for him he didn't put his hands on you."

Rachel chimes in, "I must say, I would have been upset too. Spitting on somebody is disgusting. I doubt I would ever do it."

"Were you that mad that he beat Eric up?" Ilesha asks.

"No, I was enraged because Kevin told me he had sex with another woman while I was in Jersey over the weekend," I say.

"Kevin is wrong for that. He didn't have to do you like that. He should have been straight forward with you if he wasn't happy or wanted some other sex. I'm shocked by his actions," says Rachel.

"Bitch please. I'm not. I will never be shocked by a man cheating. He probably took one of them lil "thots" home from the Halloween party. There were a lot of them in there, but I made them look nonexistent. All men just want a nut," states Ilesha.

"Aww, if you felt the urge to spit on him, he must have really hurt you. I feel for you. You didn't need him anyway. He's the loser in my book," Rachel says.

"Yeah, she's right. That's not like you to lose your cool over being cheated on. I've seen you brush off worse like it never even happened. You must be jealous," Ilesha says.

I reply, "Girl, please! I wasn't jealous that he cheated. I am a little mad at the way he threw it in my face. He didn't even have to mention it. I didn't like that he was intentionally trying to hurt me, so I spit in his face."

"I understand girl. That could've been one

of those things he just took to his grave with him. Sometimes it's better to just keep your business to yourself," Rachel says.

"Then he went even further to tell me that her sex is better than mine. Had the audacity to say that I could take some lessons from the female. I damn near lost it on him at that point," I reply.

"Well damn, he didn't say who she is, did he?" asks Ilesha.

"No, he didn't unfortunately. All he said is that I know her and she resembles me," I reply.

"It's really not important anyway. That would be one more level of drama that you don't need. You know if you knew who she was, you'd want to confront her. I think you should focus on your boys and maybe repairing things with Eric," narrates Ilesha.

"Sheena, I agree with her. That is really a minor detail. Who she is doesn't matter. The fact that he did it is really all that matters. And the way he did it. You just don't need to deal with him romantically again. Unfortunately, he does have to be in your life because of Devin," Rachel comments.

"I know girls. You're absolutely right. I'll put it on the back burner," I say.

The sad part of all of this is that I know they are right that it doesn't matter who he slept with. What really matters is that I have the information I need to let him go. Unfortunately, it does matter to me. I'm curious to know who is fine enough for him to have cheated on me with. Hell, I'm deeply interested in what female has better loving than me. My goods were well enough to serve two men simultaneously, so I know I'm sitting on a gold mine. I knew my fantasy wouldn't last forever, but it still bothers me. These were *my* relationships to end.

This is going to drive me crazy. I have to know who this mystery woman is. Should I tell my girls that I want to find out who she is? What will they think if I tell them I really need to know her identity? I could just ask Kevin who she is and that'll be it. Wait, that's probably what he wants me to do. I refuse to give him the satisfaction of knowing that I'm interested in knowing who she is.

I hope for Kevin's and this mystery woman's sake that he is lying. I wouldn't care about him cheating with a stranger because I expect men to be disloyal, but if he cheated with someone I know, that's different. The offense of cheating is worse to me because it becomes personal. I will take that as a personal attack against me. No woman should ever sleep with her friend's man. That's a violation of epic proportions.

If I find out who she is, she will have hell to pay. She can't possibly think that I would let her get away with such a vile act. I don't like to be this way, but if I have to, I will. I will hurt both of them. The thought of the two of them fucking around behind my back infuriates me. I hope I don't have to send anybody to the hospital.

"Of course, we're right. He's probably just jealous over the night you spent with Eric and wants you to be jealous like he is. Girl, rest your mind. He didn't fuck anybody," Ilesha states.

"That is an interesting theory Ilesha has. It's very plausible for him to have concocted this fictitious story just to make you mad. It has to be considered," Rachel states.

"I know. I know. I still think I'm gonna hold it to be true and I'm even gonna look into it," I report.

"How are you going to look into it? You do know that's going to be a daunting task?" Ilesha asks.

Rachel states, "I don't think you should waste your time with a hunt for a needle in a haystack."

"I hear you, but nothing is impossible. The world isn't so big when you know where to look. I only have to go to In the Mix," I say.

Rachel eventually supports my decision to try to find out who the woman Kevin cheated with is. However, Ilesha isn't supportive. According to her, it is a complete waste of time and doesn't change anything. It's my situation and I have to get to the bottom of it. I need to devise a plan to find out what I need to know.

I need to know if he actually cheated or if he's just jealous and made the story up. Our relationship can recover from a lie, but if he truly fucked another woman, it's over. I can't deal with that. I can't. As far as getting Eric back, I can make that go my way too. It may take a small amount of ingenuity on my part, but I know my skills will enable me to make it happen. I have to employ another strategy to put the broken pieces of my life back together.

Where is my phone? It's time to brainstorm a series of actions that I can take to get me in the know. I know somebody at In the Mix saw something that night. I type some things I can do and now it's time to get on my grind.

CHAPTER 11
Sheena's Perspective

I'm going to In the Mix tonight. I don't feel like staying in and I have business to handle. The only question is flats or stilettos? I'm going with stilettos tonight. In the Mix is having their normal "Wild Wednesday" night mixer. I'm riding solo tonight. I'm not including my girls for this outing. They don't even know that I'm hanging out tonight. I normally don't go out without them because it's just not safe, but since I'm not drinking tonight, I feel that I'll be okay. I just want to be seen.

I take two selfies before I leave the house and post them to Instagram. My caption reads, "Killin it". I know I'm looking great tonight. I wonder how many men will approach me while I'm out. I plan to be very social and entertaining. This tight red dress tells everyone looking that

I'm fierce and full of passion. One last wardrobe check in the mirror and I leave the house. I must admit that my legs look quite exquisite.

I pull into the parking lot and summon the valet attendant over to my car. I get out the car, take the valet ticket, and walk into the club. I know better than to park my car on the street and walk over here by myself. Thank God for valet parking.

I go to the restroom to ensure my outfit hasn't malfunctioned during the drive over. I am good to go. When I walk out of the restroom, there are several men looking in my direction. One guy motions as if he's drinking a drink. He is asking me if I want a drink. I shake my head no, but I call him over. He's alright looking, but my main purpose for him is to keep me occupied for a few minutes.

We exchange names and chat for a few minutes. He is so dry and uninteresting. He asks me repeatedly if I want a drink. I turn him down each time. I feel bad because I don't even remember his name. Kyle, Keith, or Kirk is his name, I think. If someone offered me a million dollars to say his name, I'd lose the money. His name should be Forgettable. We converse for a few minutes longer and then I dismiss him.

On to the next. As I scan the venue, I see a familiar face and I approach him. I haven't seen him since one of those business classes in college. What's his name again? His name is Clyde. I'm sure that's it. He was fantastic when it came to numbers and math. Clyde smiles as I approach him and stands to give me a hug. We play a quick game of catchup. He tells me that he's in real estate. I would be lying if I said I'm surprised. That is his calling. Clyde is my boy, so I offer to buy him a drink.

I hope he doesn't think that I'm interested in him. This drink I'm buying him is because he's a real cool dude and because I know all these guys are watching me. I take a picture with Clyde draped all over me and post the picture to social media. I know every picture I take will end up being seen by Kevin and Eric. They unquestionably will be green with envy. That's part of my plan. I don't wait for men; men wait for me. I tell Clyde that it's great seeing him and then I part ways with him.

What's next? I go to the DJ and ask him to play a line dancing song. I know most dudes in here will leave the dance floor when the song drops. The Electric Slide comes on and the dance floor nearly empties of all the guys. I don't mind the ladies flooding the floor because I will stand out amongst them. I need the guys off the floor, so they can see me and talk about what they would do to me sexually.

All men look around clubs to see who's the prettiest or sexiest woman and discuss how they would do this and that to her. Men are such heathens and their actions are so predictable. It doesn't take much to turn their heads. The problem they face is that they think with the wrong head. I also don't want any of these men trying to grind on me, so line dancing is perfect to prevent that from happening.

Why is this guy motioning me to come here? Can't he see that I'm clearly doing the Electric Slide? I shake my head in the "no" direction and continue dancing. I turn my body to keep up with the direction the Electric Slide mandates. Next, I feel somebody trying to dance up on me. How the hell can someone try to dance with a person during the Electric Slide? I look back and see the same guy who was telling me to come over. He is really attempting to ride me when this is soooo not the song to be grinding to. In my opinion, this is a solo dance. The Electric Slide isn't for partners.

I spin to the beat of the song and see Sage standing a few feet away from the dance floor. I knew it was only a matter of time before he came for me. I know he's annoyed by all of these guys in here getting my attention. I only entertained them, so he could see me and become a little jealous. His timing is impeccable because I was about to give this guy trying to dance with me some choice words. I blow Sage a kiss while dancing and he catches it. He catches the kiss I blew him and puts it to his lips.

I know I have him right where I want him. I know he will blow the kiss back at me because he is surprised that I even blew him one in the first place. As I figure, Sage returns my air kiss. I gently cradle his air smooch and rub it on my sweet spot. Sage winks and nods his head as if to say he likes where I placed his kiss. Sage points to the bar. I finish my dance and prance to the bar to talk to him.

"I would ask you if you want a drink, but I've seen you turn down too many, so I know you aren't drinking tonight," Sage says.

I flip my hair behind my ear and reply, "No, no drinks for me tonight. I'm just out by myself having a good time, so I can't drink tonight."

I knew he was watching me from the moment I walked into the bar. I was banking on it. I know he still yearns for my touch and attention. I don't want to sit at the bar and talk, so I have to say something to enable me to get to Sage's office without being too obvious.

"Hey, I noticed you smiled when I placed your air kiss on my sweet spot," I say.

Sage replies, "Damn right I did. You know you can get that anytime you want."

I act like I can't hear what Sage said. I tell him that it's too loud. I know he wants me in the back anyway, so I know he'll ask me to come to the back. He doesn't utter another word and motions me to his office. I love it when a plan comes together. We go to his office and have some small talk.

"I heard the Halloween party was pretty live.

Everybody, even my girls, was talking about it. Like nonstop," I say.

Sage replies proudly, "Yeah, it was a great turnout. More people came out than expected. We were packed all night. We really cashed in and there weren't any major problems. There was only one downside to the night."

"Really, what was that?" I ask.

"The only problem I had that night was that you weren't there," says Sage.

I'm not surprised he said that. He is a master of words and slick come backs. I know he just wants to flatter me because he wants some more of me. He always tells me that we aren't over. I don't know where he gets that notion from. I wish I would have stayed for the party after what Kevin did. If I were here, he would have never had a fling with some "thot".

I reply, "I'm sure you didn't miss me too much. I hear there were plenty of beautiful women in attendance. You weren't worried about me because you were focused on the other eye candy. I know you had the ladies drooling over you."

"That's what you think, but it's not true. I've slowed down considerably over the last year. It was time to grow up and be a man," Sage narrates.

"Right, I'll believe that when I see it," I say.

Sage replies, "I'm gonna show you. No more games. I'm serious."

"I just want you to show me some pictures from the party. My girls told me the costumes were outta this world. I saw some on the club website, but I'm sure that's not all of them," I say.

Sage takes me over to his computer and opens up a file that contains all of the pictures taken by the photographer he always hires for the Halloween parties. I really don't care about any of these people's costumes except one. I am on a hunt for whoever Kevin slept with. Sage stands over me and chats while I execute my search. Whatever he's saying is going in one ear and out the other. I wish he would just go back out in the bar and leave me alone.

"Sage, go get me an ice water. My throat is dry. I don't think I've had anything to drink since I got here," I say.

Sage grants my request and goes to get my drink. I hope he doesn't come right back. Unfortunately, there are hundreds of pictures for me to look through. I have to get through all of these pictures tonight because I don't want to come back to finish looking through them. If I do come back, Sage may know I'm up to something. Before I look through all of the pictures, Sage returns with Ilesha and Rachel.

"I see somebody is out without her two best friends tonight. Bitch, don't get cursed out," warns Ilesha.

"What are you two doing here?" I ask.

"We saw the pictures you posted, so we

figured we would come out and keep you company. You know it's dangerous being out by yourself. We were worried about you," explains Rachel.

Sage has a seat in his lounge chair. Rachel and Ilesha look at the pictures with me. They have no idea what I'm up to. I'm frustrated because they want me to stop and look at every picture. I only need to look at certain pictures in detail. I have to let them know what's going on. If I don't, we'll be in here all night.

I can text them both to let them know my true motives, but Sage may pick up on something being funny if they both look at their phones at the same time. I won't risk it.

"Sage baby, I'm hungry. You should be a sweetheart and fix me a grilled chicken salad. I'm starving," I say.

Sage leaves to fix my salad. He is being very nice tonight. He must really want me back. Hell, I don't know why he wouldn't.

"Ooh girl. Look at her shoes. She's the one with the fake red bottoms I told you about," says Ilesha as she points and laughs.

I reply, "It doesn't matter because she isn't light skinned. I only care about the light skinned females in these pictures."

Rachel asks, "What are you talking about girl? What are you up to?"

I explain to them that I am looking for all of the light skinned women who were here on

Halloween night. The woman Kevin claims he slept with is my complexion, so this is my best chance of finding her. Rachel starts studying the pictures with me.

Ilesha states, "People are wearing costumes. You won't be able to see most of their faces. Girl, you are wasting your time. Just relax."

"No, I won't stop. Sage makes everybody take their masks off if they have one on. He does it for security purposes, so if someone acts up they can be identified. That's why he takes pictures. He told me that when we were dating," I explain.

Rachel says, "That's smart, but he didn't make Ilesha take her mask off."

I say, "That woulda been like him telling me to take my mask off. He knows her, so he probably didn't sweat it because of that."

"I wasn't taking it off regardless of his security plan. My outfit was popping and wasn't getting messed up for anyone," Ilesha says.

We laugh at her because she is dead serious. She would have given Sage hell if he would have told her to remove the mask. Rachel and I look through the pictures while Ilesha sits down and relaxes. She clearly doesn't want any part of the search. I guess this is a bit far-fetched.

"What will you do if you find out who she is? Are you gonna whoop her ass?" Ilesha asks.

"That's a great question. I don't know what I'll do, but I'll cross that bridge when I come to it.

For now, I just need these pictures," I say.

"Okay, you'll have the pictures, but you still won't have their names. You need names to put with the pictures. Girl, you are killing me," Ilesha explains.

"Honey, she's right. It's not like you can find them here. They may only have come here for the party. Contacting them will be impossible," Rachel chimes in.

"Let me worry about that. Trust me, I know what I'm doing," I say.

I end up coming to Rachel's and Ilesha's picture. I call Ilesha over to look at the picture, but she refuses to do so. She leaves the office to go to the bar. Rachel and I continue to look through the pictures together. We eventually get through all of the pictures and I now have more to help me with my search. Sage comes back into the office with my salad just as we finish. I eat some of my salad to make it look like I really want it. We chat with Sage for a while before we leave the office.

"Thanks for everything Sage. Tonight was cool. I think I'll stop through tomorrow after I leave the gym. I may bring my girls with me, so you don't try anything," I say.

"Trust me they won't stop anything I want to do to you. You should know that about me by now," Sage retorts. "I hope you stop by though."

We say our goodbyes and leave. Ilesha is at the bar, so we wait for her to finish her drink and

117

we walk outside. Rachel pokes fun at me because she feels that I'm falling for Sage again. I let her know that I'm not big on Sage, but she doesn't believe me. I tell her that we are going to come back tomorrow because I need her help.

CHAPTER 12
Sheena's Perspective

I go home and jump in the bed. I have the first piece to solving this intricate puzzle. There were only six females in the pictures that fit the description Kevin gave me. I'm going back to In the Mix with Rachel tomorrow. I know Sage is happy about that. My mind is racing all over the place. Kevin, Eric, my sons, work, and everything else are infiltrating my thoughts. I close my eyes and try to block it all out. I have to get some sleep.

My phone alarm goes off seemingly too soon. There is no way it's time to get up already. Finding sleep last night was an arduous task. I tossed and turned all night. I know part of my not sleeping well is because I'm a little stressed and the other reason is because I need some sexual healing. I haven't gone this long without sex, since before I first had sex with Kevin. I think I'm having withdrawals. My peach is throbbing profusely. I need some dick to relieve some of this stress.

Let me get out this bed and get my day started. I need this shower to energize me. After I shower, I skype my mom in Jersey, so I can see my boys. Seeing them makes me feel a little better, actually a lot better. I love my boys. They are my inspiration and I'll have their backs no matter what happens with their fathers. Hopefully, their fathers don't turn into just sperm donors because my relationship with them is tarnished. Either way, I'll make sure my boys are well taken care of. I know my girls will support me if I need it. They are the boys' godmothers; it's their duty. I chat with my mom and bundles of joy and cheer up. I'm not as rattled as I was before I skyped with them. Knowing they are healthy and happy calms me down. Plus, I couldn't be rattled while talking to them. I have to separate my outside affairs from my mommy affairs.

I pull up at my business. As soon as I walk through the door, I'm informed of a bouquet of flowers that have been delivered for me. It's probably from Eric. I know he wants to make up for the other day. I really don't see why he was so mad at me. The arrangement is beautifully filled with my favorite flower, the iris. I hope he knows it will take more than an arrangement to win me over.

I look for the card to see what sweet message he has left. I find the card and tear it open. The card reads "Thinking of you" and that's it. It isn't signed with a name. I don't even recognize the handwriting on it. I ask my assistant who delivered the package. I hope it was someone other than a delivery service. Unfortunately, my assistant informs me that it was delivered by an employee of the florist.

So much for knowing who sent them. Either way, they are very pretty, so I sit them on my desk. I should call Eric to confirm if he sent them. No, I'll wait for him to call or text me. He'll be wondering if I got them and eventually call me. I can't help but to take a selfie with these flowers. I know if I post a picture with me and the flowers, a couple of things will happen. One thing that'll indubitably happen is whoever sent them will make a positive comment about them. Secondly, whoever didn't send them will be jealous about it and comment to that effect.

I'm all for playing the jealousy card. Many people think it's a bit childish, but hell, it works for me. If you play your cards the right way, you'll win every time and I'm all about winning. I post the picture with me and my flowers. I immediately receive a bunch of likes and comments. Unfortunately, they are not from Eric. Maybe he didn't send them or maybe he's at work and hasn't been on social media to see my picture. Somebody's going to be in their feelings very soon. It's just a matter of who. You better believe it won't be me.

Work is smooth. I love owning my own business. I can close my door whenever I feel like it and stay to myself. I don't have to check with anybody if I don't want to come into the office. Today, I even steal a nap while I'm in my office. I needed it after all of that broken sleep I had last night.

I have worked enough for the day and I don't have anything else pressing, so I go home. Rachel is coming over at six o'clock, so we can hang out again. Ilesha is busy tonight and won't be joining us. I know Rachel's going to be early like always, so I start getting ready as soon as I get home. I miss going out like this.

Rachel shows up at quarter til six. I'm ready to go when she rings the bell, so I grab my clutch and head out the door. There is no need for Rachel to come in. That would be a waste of time.

Rachel comments, "Someone's in a hurry tonight. You must be in a rush to see your new-old boo!"

"Child please. I know you aren't talking about Sage. I'm not in a rush to see him or anybody. I'm just punctual and don't see why being on time has to be about a man," I reply.

"You're right. It just seemed like you two were pretty friendly last night. He was waiting on you hand and foot. Hanging on your every word and want," Rachel says.

"Yeah, I noticed that too, but I'm not thinking about him. He is tired. Old news as they say. Sage blew his shot with me a long time ago," I explain.

Rachel remarks, "I know what you mean. Things were pretty ugly between you two, but you know people have the capacity to change. We were young when all that stuff happened. Besides, you are single again, so you are free to do whatever you want."

I reply, "Don't remind me about being single. I really shouldn't be. I'm supposed to be married with children and just enjoying life. Instead, I'm horny, manless, and extremely curious to find out who my ex slept with. Sad times, but it's okay."

We pull up to the lounge and go inside. I hope tonight goes the way I anticipate. Sage is waiting to see me, I'm sure. I'll play it cool and not go speak to him. He'll seek us out for certain. He's probably in the back looking at the cameras to see who comes in. There is no coincidence that he always comes from the back shortly after we arrive. He is a borderline stalker. Sage comes to us almost immediately. I know he was anxiously awaiting my arrival. I give him an extended hug and a kiss on the cheek. I know he is both happy and surprised by my greeting. I have no reason not to entertain him now. I am single all over again. It wasn't that long ago when

I was living the dream. I had everything I wanted and life was bliss. However, that's not the case now. I have a mission. I need to find out who Kevin cheated with.

"Ladies, I have your normal table ready. I kept it open just in case. I was beginning to think you weren't gonna make it tonight. Time was ticking by. Figured you decided to stay in," says Sage.

I verbalize, "You know I keep my word. I told you I'd be by and here I am. You know I wanted to see you again. Last night was fun cooling here. It reminded me of old times."

"I agree. Last night was cool. We had a million good nights in here. They don't have to end. We can create many more. No need to stop now," Sage orates.

I reply, "That's why we are here now. Another fun night is before us. I'm ready."

"I'm all for a good night. My staff knows your meals and drinks are on the house, so enjoy. I have to run to the office to take care of a few things," Sage comments and then steps away.

I need to get back into the office because I still have more snooping to do. Unfortunately, I can't have Sage in there while I'm doing my thing. Rachel is going to have to help me get him out of his office.

"Rachel, you know what you need to do, right? Tell Sage you need to chat with him for a minute and pull him into the bar. Inform him that you want to throw me a surprise party for my birthday and you need his insight on how to possibly set it up," I explain. "Remember to wait about five minutes to come to his office to talk to him."

I know Sage will be happy to be a part of the birthday planning process. He'll be thinking that he can get brownie points for helping to make the party a success. I told Rachel to ask as many questions as possible. I even gave her a little script to follow. I'm sure she'll come through for me because my girls never let me down. I walk to Sage's office and stand in the doorway.

"Sage, speaking of good times, I wanna look at some more pictures from the Halloween party. I didn't get through all of them. The flicks I saw were really nice!" I say.

Sage replies, "Yeah, it was a very nice night. You can use the same computer from last night."

I go back to the work station and pretend like I'm looking at the photos. Rachel will be in here any minute to remove Sage from his office and then I can really get down to business.

"I may not be the sharpest pencil in the box, but I know a scam when I see one. Sheena, you can't put one over on me. I wrote the book on being gamed," Sage says.

I know he can't possibly know why I'm in his office. He's sharp, but damn, he isn't a mind reader. I'll play like I don't know what he's talking about.

"Sage, what are you talking about?" I ask.

"Don't play dumb with me. I know that you didn't come to this office to look at some pictures. You're back in here to see me, so you can cut the charade," Sage says.

"Maybe I am. If I am, do you mind?" I ask.

I know responding this way is intriguing to Sage. He loves anything that is like battle of the wits. He can't resist a challenge of the minds. He wants to see if he can get an answer out of me without me knowing it. While we are conversing, there is a knock at the door. I know it's Rachel and she's right on time.

"Come in," I say.

"Oh, let me guess. You came in to rescue your friend, didn't you?" Sage asks.

"If that's your guess, you are wrong. I actually came in here to get your opinion on something. Let me run a few ideas through you. I want to see what you think about a way to setup a section of your bar that may increase revenue," Rachel states.

Rachel is silky smooth. She knows she couldn't walk in and say she needed him for my surprise birthday party plans with me sitting here. Instead, she came up with a ruse on the fly to get him into the bar. Sage rose to his feet as soon as Rachel mentioned increased revenue. Sage is definitely about his money, so I'm sure he'll be disappointed when Rachel starts talking about birthday plans.

As soon as he clears the door, I run to Sage's desk and begin to search through it. I need to find the cards that everybody had to fill out on Halloween. Sage is very meticulous and his record keeping is flawless. He makes every person take a photo as well as put their contact information on a card for the best costume contest. I can match the card with the photos and find the mystery woman Kevin slept with.

I check his desk and don't see the information cards. I know he hasn't gotten rid of the cards yet because he normally holds them for months after the party. Maybe they're in his file cabinet. I open up cabinet after cabinet and don't see them. Damn, finding these cards is my only hope of locating this woman. I want to know who is supposedly finer than me and has better pussy than me. There were some pretty girls at the party, but none of them come close to me in beauty. Ilesha was the best looking one at the party by far.

Kevin claims that I know the female he cheated with. I recognize a few of the females from the photos I looked through. Man I need to find where Sage put those info cards. I'll be able to put a face with a name and costume. I check the closet in his office for the info, but they're not in there either. I know Rachel won't be able to keep Sage occupied for too much longer, so my luck needs to change immediately.

I have to think like Sage. What makes the

most sense? Where would he put the raffle information? I hope he didn't throw them away. I sit at Sage's desk to see if I can get into his head. Fortunately, I have a stroke of luck. I see a folder under his planner labeled Halloween party. My eyes almost pop out of my skull because I know this is what I'm looking for.

I quickly snatch the folder like a mother would snatch a child who's about to run in front of a moving vehicle. I reach in my pocket and pull out the names of the costumes I pulled off the website from Halloween. Now, I should be able to match the costumes the females wore with their names. It's crazy how this folder contains the information I need and was under my nose the entire time. I almost missed it, but I didn't.

Let me see who I know. I look through the folder to check the names. I see several names of women I know who are light skinned like me. I exclude Ilesha immediately because I know it's not even a possibility that she's the woman Kevin slept with. I get three names of the ladies who appear on the list I pulled off the website. I have three more to find. My plan is yielding the results I hoped for.

As I continue my search, Sage appears back in his office. I know I'm caught at this point. I really have no reason to be at his desk searching through his files. I have to play this just right. He won't know what hit him.

"Sheena, what are you doing at my desk

rummaging through my folders?" Sage asks.

I respond, "Your perception is a bit misaligned. I am not rummaging through your stuff, I'm reminiscing."

"Is that right? About what exactly?" Sage inquires.

"I'm thinking about when I would be in here helping you with your books for the club and then you'd come in and walk up behind me and nibble on my ear. Then you would tell me how beautiful I am. Hell, before long, we'd both be naked and going at it," I explain.

Sage immediately is pulled in by my comments. He has forgotten that I'm clearly looking through his paperwork. It's pretty simple to play a man. You can distract him by either stroking his ego or by mentioning sex. All he wants to talk about now is sexing me. I entertain his advances for a moment. I have to keep the focus off of me snooping through his stuff.

"You know you are the best I ever had," I say.

"You mean out of all the guys you ever slept with, I'm the best? Like absolutely the best?" Sage asks.

Now, it's time to really get him. Men care way too much about their dicks. If a man lost his dick, he'd probably kill himself. Why do they think sex is the only thing that matters? He totally misses the fact that he is the man who hurt me the most. Sage never wants to recognize that or go into any detail about it.

"Yes, the best ever. Don't try to play me like there have been a million men in my sex life though. The way you touch me and stroke me is like no other. My body tingles when you're in me. I still get the feeling of excitement in my stomach every time I see you," I say.

I know I'm laying it on thick, but this is what it takes to throw a man off balance. He walks over to me and glides his hand slowly up my thigh until it rests in the cradle of my back. He's standing right behind me and leans in to nibble on my neck.

He softly kisses my neck, my shoulders, and collar bone. Sage knows how to navigate my body and treats me like a delicate flower. He moves his hand further down to gently caress and grasp my ass. I turn around, place my hand on his chest, and look him in his eyes. He thinks he has me. Sage pulls me closer, sweeps my hair out of my face, and grabs the back of my neck. I'm in control. He moves his head down and guides my head upward with his hand on the back of my neck. Just before our lips meet, I look down and tell him we need to take things slow. Did he really think it was going to be that easy?

I tell him to go get Rachel for me. At this point, he is putty in my hands and will do whatever I say. I want him to get Rachel, so I can finish searching and so he won't try to make any more sexual advances on me. Not that I would normally mind, but that's not what I need right now. I need to finish the task at hand.

I find the last three names that I'm looking for. Rachel and Sage walk in right after I put the folder back. All three of us chat for a while. I'm ready to go because I have what I want now. I tell Sage that it's time for Rachel and me to leave. Sage walks us out of his office and asks when he'll be able to spend some time with me.

"My life is very complicated right now, so I don't know at this time. I'll keep you posted though," I reply.

Sage replies, "I understand. We all live busy lives. Not as simple as things were in college. Running this club keeps me busy too. Just don't forget about me."

"I couldn't possibly forget about my first love," I say.

Sage smiles immediately. I give him a kiss on the cheek before we leave. I have to keep him close because I may need him now that I'm single. There's nothing wrong with calling on an ex to scratch an itch once in a while. He'll deliver the goods the way I need them to be delivered.

CHAPTER 13
Sheena's Perspective

I keep the departure conversation short with Rachel because I'm more than eager to put this puzzle together. I drive home disregarding all reasonable driving practices. It astonishes me how all logic gets thrown out of the window when people are on a mission. I'm glad I made it home without getting a ticket. I am so guilty of driving recklessly, but you know what, I don't care. I should go on Instagram now to hit these girls up.

I, Sheena Mills, am about to do the one thing I always said I wouldn't do. I'm about to contact these females via social media and confront them. Hell, somebody has to give me some answers. I do feel bad for the women I'm going to bother who haven't done anything to deserve my accusations, but I have no other options at this point. Should I come off aggressive or assertive? Maybe I should befriend them and try to have a nice conversation about what happened after the Halloween party.

I clearly have some more brainstorming to do. My approach may determine the outcome of my results. I need more opinions, so I guess I won't be contacting any of the potential mistresses tonight. I'll hit my girls up tomorrow and see what they think. Conversing with them will afford me every option available to me. My mind is all over the place. I still need to deal with Eric and our situation. One problem at a time is what I'll handle. I'm not trying to fight five fires at once. It's late and I'm tired. This shower will be a quick one. Hopefully, it relaxes me a little bit. After my shower, I plop down on my bed and drift into a deep slumber.

I wake up before my alarm even chimes. I'm on an internal clock right now. I need to text Rachel and Ilesha to see if they can come through, so we can see what my next move should be. I grab my phone and send a group text to them. We converse via text message.

I text, *Hey.*

Rachel texts back, *Hi, my sister. How'd it go once you got home?*

Morning bitches. It's too early for all this texting. Woke my ass up. How'd what go? Ilesha texts.

Girl, you're so abrasive. It's too early for you to be swearing, Rachel texts back.

I reply, *You two are funny, but listen I need you both to come over at about one.*

Umm, I'll be there, but don't act like I didn't ask a question though. How'd what go? Ilesha texts.

Sheena found a little info about Kevin and his infidelity. That's all, Rachel texts.

I text, *Yeah, so come over so we can make sense of this like we always do. See you in a little while. Thanks huns.*

I begin making lunch for me and the girls. They always appreciate when I cook for them. It's the least I can do for interrupting their lives once again. With the way they always come to my rescue, I should take them on vacation, but today, they will have to settle for salad and finger foods. We don't need anything too heavy anyway. My phone starts ringing a few minutes before one. It must be Rachel telling me that she's outside. I know it's not Ilesha because it's too early for her to arrive. To my surprise, it's Eric calling me. I decide not to answer his call. He is on knock off for a minute. He should have been more supportive the other day when he and Kevin fought. It's not my fault he got his ass handed to him.

My doorbell chimes as I send Eric's call to voicemail. Maybe Eric is at the door. It's not out of his character to pop up on me especially, since he is all in his feelings right now. I sneak a peek out of the window to see who it is. Fortunately, it's Rachel. I didn't feel like dealing with Eric and his emotions right now. I let Rachel in and before I close the door, Ilesha pulls up. We don't believe it's her, since she's early.

As Ilesha comes through the door I say, "Didn't expect you to be here this early. Something must be wrong with you girl."

Ilesha waves a bottle of Cîroc in the air and replies, "Something is wrong with me. I'm not drunk yet. Get me a glass."

Me and Rachel shake our heads and burst out laughing. We surely go to the kitchen and get a few glasses out. Hell, we want to drink too. I need at least one drink to ease my nerves, so I can think straight. Ilesha wants to drink for no other reason than it being fun. Rachel must want to be freaky with her man. The drinks will give her some courage. We enjoy our drinks, food, and conversation.

"Here's the situation. I have the girls' names from the Halloween party and matched them with their costumes and social media info. I wanna know how I should proceed from here," I report.

"I don't think you should contact them at all. He is lying to make you mad like he is. You know misery loves company. Don't put too much into what he's saying. Nobody would be stupid enough to tell on themselves. Shit, I know I wouldn't," Ilesha explains.

"I think he did something. I don't think he would put himself in the hot seat for nothing.

Now that would just be senseless. He was most likely mad about Eric and thought that cheating was the best way to retaliate," Rachel comments.

"Rachel, I agree. Kevin said that I know her, so it makes sense. He made it personal because he knows I would want to know who the girl is," I reply.

"I really don't want anything to do with this hunt, but I'll help because you need me. Let me see the names you have for your witch hunt," says Ilesha.

I hand Ilesha the list. Ilesha and Rachel both peruse the list of names. Next, they go to my computer to look at the pictures of the women on In the Mix's website. I pour us some more drinks while they look things over. We talked Kevin up because he's calling now, but I send him to voicemail.

Ilesha asks, "You have Mia on this list? You know that's totally not her character right?"

Rachel says, "You can positively take Mia off the list. She's beautiful and I'm sure all the guys in there wanted her, but she wouldn't do that."

"Besides, she was with her hubby all night. They left together. It's not likely that she left with her husband, went home, and then left out to go fuck Kevin. Take her off the list," Ilesha reports.

"Okay, okay I'll remove her as a suspect. That's why I wanted you guys here. You two were there and were privy to what I missed.

Keep going," I say.

"I don't intend to be vile, but these two ladies just aren't pretty enough. Based on the way you look and his ex-girlfriends you've shown us, I don't think he would have sex with them," says Rachel.

"It's definitely not either one of them. I can say that with certainty," Ilesha states.

Ilesha pulls out her phone and shows me a video of the two females who I feel are possible suspects. It's a video of them at Stadium, a popular strip club in D.C. The video shows the two ladies fighting at the strip club and being arrested by the police. Needless to say, I take them off of my list of suspects.

That's even better for me because this leaves fewer females for me to contact. Unfortunately, they weren't able to eliminate any more. Rachel feels like the other three ladies could be choices. Ilesha still wants me to stop what I'm doing.

"Now that it's narrowed down, I have to think of a clever way to approach finding out which one it is. I have a few different ways to go about it. I can be friendly and try to get the truth out of her or I can be rude and hope she tells me out of anger," I say.

Rachel says, "Be friendly to her. That will keep the drama from escalating. There's no need to make matters worse. If you are mean and rude, she may want to become violent. You'll have a new issue to deal with."

I'm not surprised by her response. She is never confrontational. I'm sure Ilesha is going to say curse the women out and threaten them. I am all for what makes the most sense. Maybe I'll curse one out and be nice to the others and see where this takes me.

Ilesha says, "I really don't see any of that working. I think you should let it go. Let's be honest, you were fucking both Kevin and Eric, so you had to know one of them would seek revenge. Normal human reaction."

"Ilesha, why are you so against me trying to get to the bottom of this? Are you saying Kevin was justified in his actions?" I ask.

"Sheena, all I'm saying is karma is a bitch. Besides, the male ego is very fragile, so once it's damaged; you have to be ready for anything from a man. Very unpredictable creatures," Ilesha says.

"I agree totally. They're not as emotionless as they act. You can take a man down with one slight blow to his ego," Rachel narrates.

"But to answer your question I'd be nice to them. If you are disrespectful, they may put up a defensive wall and not let you in. If you are polite, you may gain her respect as a woman and get your answers. I'm just saying," Ilesha says.

"You both say friendly, so friendly it is. I'd rather that anyway. I don't like being rude to people unless my hand is forced," I say.

"Yes, we know how you get when you are rattled. I still can't believe you slapped Kevin the night Kevin and Eric found out about each other. Girl, you are a mess," says Rachel.

Ilesha says, "I'm gonna leave you to your business. I have to go now."

Rachel asks in a concerned voice, "Honey, what's wrong?"

"After drinking that Cîroc, I need some dick in my life. The kitty cat is twitching and throbbing. She needs to be invaded. I gotta go get some," Ilesha responds.

Rachel is overcome with embarrassment. Once she digests Ilesha's response, her face turns redder than Rudolph's nose. Rachel knows that she asked the wrong question. I laugh because I know the feeling. I love having tipsy trysts. I could go for some sex myself.

My phone starts ringing. I look at the screen and it's Eric calling again. Rachel and Ilesha motion that they are leaving, but I hold them up. I answer the call and put my phone on speaker. Eric greets me and I give him a cold greeting in return.

Eric says, "I miss you baby. We need to talk and get this situation rectified."

I ask, "Oh, you miss me? You miss me or my pussy?"

Eric replies, "I miss both."

"You wanna bury your face in it like normal? You just want me to cum all over your face?" I ask.

I put the phone on mute, so he can't hear us

laughing at him. Me and the girls are laughing out of control. He is having a weak moment and we are enjoying every moment of it.

"Learn how to fight you punk bitch!" Ilesha yells out.

Fortunately, I still have the phone muted because he would have been devastated if he heard that comment. I can't stop laughing. To my surprise, Rachel is cracking up laughing too. We all have tears rolling down our faces. I purposely hit the end call button. It's no big worry because I didn't want to talk to him anyway. I only answered his call, so we could clown him. Eric sends a text stating he understands why I hung up on him and to call him whenever I feel up to talking.

He will really be eager to talk to me. I'll ignore him for a little while longer. I need to post a couple more pictures of me with other men, so he'll really be fuming. My girls leave and I take a look at the three women's Facebook pages. Yes, I'm wall watching, but it's for a reason. It's not like I'm hating on them or I'm jealous of them. I just want to know who slept with my man, well ex man.

How should I start this message? Hi, I know we haven't spoken in a while. No, I don't like that. I got it. A simple "hey girl" is a good way to start. I could just send a picture of Kevin with a message that asks if she fucked him. What am I doing? Am I losing my mind? I need to put myself in their shoes.

How would I respond to someone I know or don't know questioning me about who I'm sleeping with? I would get defensive immediately. There is no nice way to approach these women. Once I start prying into their business, there will be an argument. I'm sure of it.

I can't find anything that gives me the exact information I need. What else can I do to find out if one of these three women is the one who slept with Kevin? I need to get inside of Kevin's house. Unfortunately, we aren't on the best terms, so I can't just pop up over there and walk in. I have to get him out of his house.

Damn, the boys are out of town, so I can't use them as an excuse. Additionally, I can't use Rachel and Ilesha as I normally do. What time is it? Kevin is at work, so maybe I don't need an excuse to get him out of the house. I'll just let myself in and see what I can find.

I text Kevin, *Hey, I think it's unfortunate that our relationship is so sour now. I wanna try to get things as close to normal as we possibly can.*

Kevin replies, *Sounds good, but I'm in a meeting right now. Will call when it's over.*

That's all I need to know. I don't want to repair the relationship with Kevin. He is a womanizer with whom I don't care to consort with. I just wanted to make sure he's working today. I drive over to Kevin's house and go inside. I wonder if he had the balls to fuck her in the same damn bed where he fucked me. He probably did, so I'll start there.

I go into his room and snoop around. I wonder if Kevin or Eric snooped around my house like this when they had access. If they did, they would've been wasting their time. What am I even doing in here? I don't want to be with this man anymore and I still don't know what I'm looking for. However, I still keep rummaging through his belongings.

I decide to go to his master bathroom and check in there. While I'm in his bathroom, Kevin calls me. I don't answer because I want to finish my search uninterrupted. Next, I search the living room, but find nothing in there. My search is giving me no clues. It's time for me to leave. This is pointless.

As I'm about to leave, I remember that I have a drawer in Kevin's room that he may have put another female's clothes in. I run upstairs to his room to check my former drawer. Damn, it's empty. He must have thrown all my stuff out. I could have been doing something more productive with this time. I walk down the stairs to exit when I hear keys at the door and Kevin's voice.

Shit! I'm so glad I didn't park in the driveway. I'd be caught for sure. I run back to his room and get under the bed. What the hell is he doing here? He claimed that he was in a meeting. What a liar. Maybe this will work out better than I thought it would. If I'm lucky, he'll bring the woman he cheated with over. Then I can jump from under this bed and whoop her ass.

As Kevin comes up the stairs, I lie under the bed. I'm very nervous because if he finds me in here it will be my ass. I'm shaking like I'm on trial for murder and the jury's about to read the verdict. Kevin flops on the bed and seems to not be going anywhere anytime soon. I know I can't spend all day under this bed. I hope he doesn't stay here too long.

Kevin gets up from the bed and begins to walk back downstairs. I'm saved. The unthinkable happens as he gets halfway to the bottom of the staircase. My phone chimes alerting me to a new message. I immediately hear Kevin heading back up the steps. Damn, I should just come from under the bed now. How stupid could I be for not turning my ringer off?

I would be livid if I found someone going through my belongings after having broken into my house. What can I tell him that will suffice? He wouldn't be dumb enough to believe that I am here on good terms. Hell, I can take him cursing me out; I just hope it doesn't turn physical.

Kevin's back in his room and stops at the foot of the bed. I don't know what he's doing. Is he playing with my emotions? He sits down on the bed and breathes in deeply. Next, he stands up and then kneels down on one knee slowly.

He's just toying with me, so I decide to just come from underneath the bed. Just as I begin to slide over because I'm caught, Kevin jumps up quickly and runs to the bathroom and begins to regurgitate.

I'm grateful that I waited to make it known that I was under the bed. I almost gave myself up. I know this is my opportunity to escape. I move myself from under the bed and get the surprise of a lifetime. A red thong falls from being wedged between the mattress and the bedframe. The thong is monogrammed with the letter "I". The girl's name must start with an "I". This will help me tremendously.

I'm unsure whether I should take the thong with me or not. However, one thing that I am sure of is that I have to leave now. As I get from underneath the bed, I leave the thongs where they are and I stealthily walk to the stairs. I exit the house and make it to my car undetected.

I drive straight home and flop on the couch. Whew! That was close. I found the thong at Kevin's, but now what? That still doesn't give me much information to go on. What could this girl's name be? India, Isabel, Iesha? I don't know many people whose name starts with the letter "I" and none of the names of three final suspects even begin with the letter "I". I need more information.

I need another approach to this. I call Kevin and he answers.

"Hey, I'm gonna get straight to the point. You need to come get your belongings before this stuff ends up in the garbage and we need to discuss how you will see your son when I go to Jersey to pick him up," I say.

"When should I come by to pick the stuff up and to talk things through?" Kevin asks.

I respond, "I am thinking sometime today. The sooner, the better because I have things to do later. In fact, you need to come now."

"See, this is the shit I'm talking about. You think you run every damn thing, but you don't. Everybody is supposed to move on Sheena's time. Well, newsflash, I don't," says Kevin.

I say, "I really don't have time to go back and forth with you. Your stuff is here and will be in the dumpster soon if you don't come get it. More importantly we need to discuss the visitation situation for Devin."

Kevin is silent for a moment. I can tell he is weighing his options. He has some very expensive suits, shoes, and watches over here. I know he doesn't want to lose them. He knows that I will throw all of his belongings out without a second's hesitation.

"I'll be over in an hour," Kevin says.

I say, "Bring some boxes or bags with you."

An hour later my doorbell rings. It's Kevin and he's right on time. I'm very friendly with him. One would think that he hasn't done anything wrong.

I say, "I guess we can talk while you pack your stuff up."

Kevin walks from room to room and closet to closet collecting his things. We discuss a tentative schedule for him to pick Devin up. We really don't need the courts to handle this for us. We are both mature enough to make it work.

I say, "Damn, I was supposed to call my mom. She mentioned something about meeting me halfway to drop the boys off. Call my phone for me."

Kevin calls my phone, but it goes straight to the voicemail. He doesn't know that I hid my phone and turned it off, so I could use his phone.

"Kevin, let me use your phone to call my mom. I hope she isn't on the road already," I say.

Kevin quickly lends me his phone. I dial my phone and fake a conversation with my mother. I exit the bedroom and head downstairs while Kevin continues to pack. I immediately open up Kevin's Instagram app. Using my phone to contact the females would have been pointless, but contacting them from his phone could be very helpful.

I know I don't have all day to use his phone, so I send all three women the same message. The message reads, *Session after Halloween party was great!*

I'm hoping for immediate responses. Kevin will eventually want his phone back. It's like an eternity waiting for these women to reply. I vaguely hear Kevin calling my name, so I know he is still upstairs. I also know that he'll be coming downstairs soon.

One of the females responds back to my message. She sends back three question marks and states that it's the wrong person. Okay, one down and two to go. Damn, now Kevin is walking downstairs.

Kevin shouts as he walks down the stairs, "Sheena!"

I don't respond and just act like I don't hear him. Come on. Come on. Reply to the darn message already. If I give him his phone back before the other two women respond, my little stunt to get his phone will be a total waste. Not to mention, he'll know what I'm up to once they respond to the message I sent. He's in the living room now.

"Sheena, I need my phone," says Kevin.

I walk into the bathroom when I hear him clear the stairs. Please respond to the damn message. It doesn't take all day to see a message and reply. Everybody keeps their phone handy and the day I need quick responses they want to take all day.

"Sheena, where are you? What are you doing?" Kevin asks in a frustrated voice.

The second message finally comes through. I am so absorbed in the response that I still don't acknowledge Kevin's questions. The second female gives another negative response. She has no idea what is going on. It isn't her, so it has to be the last one. Kevin is knocking on the bathroom door.

"Just using the bathroom. I didn't think to put the phone down before I came in here. I'm sorry," I say.

Kevin says, "Well, open the door and hand me the phone. I need to use the phone for a minute."

"I'm not opening the door. That's nasty! I'm a lady. Get away from the door! I'll be out in a minute. In fact, stop talking to me," I say.

As I flush the toilet, the last message comes through. Unfortunately, her message is just like the others. She has no clue as to what my message is about. I struck out. Maybe I picked the wrong females or maybe they're denying it like Ilesha said they would. I walk out of the bathroom and hand Kevin his phone back. I wonder if I should interrogate him to find out this woman's identity. Oh well, I am going for it. I won't be able to drop this if I never find out who betrayed me.

"Kevin, we need to talk," I say.

"What's on your mind?" Kevin asks.

"I know we are not seeing eye to eye these days and that's cool because in life people don't always see eye to eye, but we need to be cordial for the sake of our son," I narrate.

"I agree we do need to have an agreeable relationship for our son's sake. The thing about it is that I'm not mad at you. You were the one who got upset with me when I told you I had sex with someone else," Kevin remarks.

"I'm glad you mentioned that because I wanted to talk to you about that also. I have to admit that I've been troubled by you claiming you slept with a friend of mine," I say.

Kevin replies, "I just told you what happened. You really shouldn't be troubled by it. It's over and what's done is done."

"Let's just be honest here. I know you just made that nonsense story up to make me mad. You can stop lying and come clean about telling me that story. I know you made it up," I say.

"Sheena, you are too full of yourself. I don't have to make up stories about who I fucked just to make you mad. I just wanted you to know that you aren't the only fish in the pond. Bottom line is I fucked your friend and she loved every minute and every stroke of it," Kevin explains.

"Well, I know your story is bullshit. I did a little research myself and none of my friends admit to sleeping with you and I believe them. My friends are extremely loyal," I report.

"Yes, they are very loyal. I do agree," Kevin retorts.

"I know they are, so cut the lies out and admit that you were just mad about Eric and me having sex without your knowledge. Be a man," I comment.

"Your friends are very loyal. Yep, loyal to themselves. I give you too much credit for being smart because you are quite stupid. I know you don't really think your friend would admit to sleeping with the father of one of your children," Kevin states.

I'm quite offended by Kevin calling me stupid. I should throw this water in his face and kick him out of my house. However, I don't see kicking him out being very productive. I will be the bigger person here. I won't tolerate another insult though. He's clearly not mad, so I have to get him emotionally involved in this conversation.

"Kevin, maybe I am stupid. If I am, I can accept that. The real issue is that you can't satisfy me the way Eric does. It seems that once you realized that, you got upset. Don't be mad at me and Eric. You should step your game up and not be so insecure," I assert.

Kevin had a very calm and arrogant demeanor up until this point of the conversation. He now has a broken look on his face and seems to be upset. I'm sure telling him that he isn't as good as Eric sexually has hurt his pride. Kevin is a very macho man, so attacking his sexual prowess is hurtful to him. He rubs his hand down his face as if that will hide his anger, but I can see the frustration building.

"Eric is better than me? That's a low blow, but I expect it from you. You are trifling just like your friends. For example, you were sleeping with me and Eric and let us run a train on you," says Kevin.

150

"Contrary to what you say, you and Eric didn't do anything to me. I set that entire situation up and you went for it. If anyone is trifling, it's you for being weak and allowing it to happen. You were the one kissing me right after I had Eric's dick in my mouth," I shoot back. "I had the best of both worlds."

"I was blinded by love and it made me do some strange things that I regret, but I don't have any bad feelings about fucking your friend. Ilesha's trifling just like you are. I'm glad she is because if she wasn't, I would have never had the opportunity to fuck her after the Halloween party. I must say she is quite the freak. Here you go thinking your friends are so loyal," Kevin reports.

"Are you saying you had sex with Ilesha?" I ask.

"That's exactly what I'm saying and her shit is years better than yours will ever be. You really need to study her moves because she is on top of her game," Kevin says.

I splash the water I'm drinking in Kevin's face. He really needs it because he is one tired ass man. He wants to break up a happy friendship with his lies. Kevin grows infuriated from the splashing of the water in his face. He lunges toward me, but I run to the other side of the island in my kitchen. Kevin quickly walks around the island in my direction. He has the face of a raging bull. I realize that I may be in over my head. I know he will pummel me with no problem, so I pick up a kitchen knife and hold it up to him.

"Get out of my face and house you liar! You disgust me more now than ever before. Hate is a strong emotion, but you are very close to being on my hate list right now. I will cut your ass if you take another step in my direction!" I scream.

"I won't come near you, but don't be mad at me because you can't handle what you dish out. She wanted to be hit with my magic stick, so I hit her with it," Kevin narrates. "I fucked you and your supposed best friend, so just deal with it."

There isn't a shot in hell that Ilesha gave him some. My girls are the most trustworthy women ever. I know he's just saying that to make me mad at her, but it's not working. Ilesha and Rachel are my "sisses from other misses" and don't have a scandalous strand of hair on their heads.

"You are a liar and it's a shame that you would try to come between us like that. I can't help it that you have low self-esteem. You were always jealous of my friendship with them anyway," I reply.

"All I can say is that I surely nutted in between the walls of her soaked pussy. I should thank you for helping me hit it. If it wasn't for you telling her how great my dick is, I probably never would've gotten to fuck her. Thanks for running your mouth," says Kevin.

"I don't want to hear any more of your garbage. You are no longer welcome in my house and you need to leave now before I hurt you," I disclose.

Kevin shrugs his shoulders and makes his way outside. I take the belongings that were packed up and throw them down the front steps. I know I should be better than this, but I can't help it. He attacked my friendship and I don't play that. I take the knife and poke holes in two of his expensive suits and cut the tongues off of his Gucci shoes. Kevin gathers his belongings and leaves my house.

CHAPTER 14
Sheena's Perspective

I immediately call Rachel and Ilesha because they need to know what's going on. I don't think this is a phone conversation, so I ask them to come to my house. Ilesha is in the middle of something, so she tells Rachel and me to come to her house. I tell Rachel that I'll pick her up from her house and we'll ride to Ilesha's house together.

When I get to Rachel's house I am still a nervous wreck. I can't stop crying. I'm not crying tears of sorrow, but I am crying tears of anger. My hands won't stop shaking. Rachel comes out of the house as soon as I pull up and gets in the car.

"These men get on my last damn nerve!" I scream as the tears roll down my face like a waterfall.

"What's wrong honey?" Rachel asks as she

gives me a sisterly embrace.

"I'll just tell you and Ilesha at the same time, so I don't have to keep telling the story over and over again. I don't want to keep reliving it," I say.

"I understand darling. I won't ask you any more questions about it. If you feel like you want to open up on the way to Ilesha's just go right ahead. You're in no shape to drive. You jump yourself in the passenger's seat and I'll drive," Rachel narrates.

We drive to Ilesha's house and I pull myself together. I don't know how I made it to Ilesha's without breaking out one of these car windows. I guess the Man upstairs calmed my nerves. Rachel and I walk into Ilesha's and are delighted by the aroma invading our nostrils. Ilesha is cooking her famous macaroni and cheese. She is in here throwing down. I guess that's why she couldn't come to my house to meet.

"Damn girl, you look a mess," says Ilesha as soon as she sees my face.

"I know. It's been another rough day. It seems like I'm having a lot of days like this lately. I just need life to get simple again," I say.

"Come in the kitchen and have a drink. We'll get through it together like we always do girl," states Ilesha.

I tell the girls that Kevin came over and things were going pretty good. I tell them about the stunt I pulled to contact the females through his Instagram page and how I snuck into his house and found a woman's thong underneath the bed. Rachel doesn't think it was a bad idea, but Ilesha feels like I am acting less than who I am. I also report that before long, Kevin and I get into a heated argument.

I say, "In the midst of the argument I threw my drink in his face because I was angry. He was totally off base with his words. I wouldn't stand for the disrespect and lies."

"Were you two talking about him cheating again?" questions Rachel.

"Girl, we were going at it. He was insulting me and I was insulting him. Hell, after I threw the drink on him, he chased me around the kitchen. I know he was gonna put his hands on me, so I grabbed a knife and told him to leave," I report.

"Are you serious? What the hell happened over there?" asks Ilesha.

"He started talking about cheating on me again and I lost it," I say.

"Baby, you already knew he cheated, so what was so different about the information?" asks Rachel.

"It's not that he cheated. It's who he claims he cheated with that made me splash the drink on him," I respond. "I was disgusted."

"Well damn, who was it? Was it a prostitute? Was it another man?" asks Ilesha.

"He actually had the gumption to tell you who it was?" asks Rachel.

"Yeah, and he was rather haughty about it. That's why I got so angry and disgusted. He told me that he fucked Ilesha. I knew he was lying and I was so mad that he would lie on one of you that I just splashed him with my drink. I didn't know what else to do," I explain.

"He fucked who? He said he fucked me? You mean another Ilesha right?" asks Ilesha as she jumps out of her chair.

Rachel starts crying. She is upset that Kevin is being so evil and trying to destroy our sisterhood. Ilesha is infuriated. She's seemingly more upset than I am. She wants to get her boyfriend to beat him down, but I cut that short. He is the father of one of my sons. I can't have him hurt. Even if we aren't together, he still has to go to work.

"I want to curse him out. I know men lie on their dicks all the time, but I never had a man lie on my pussy. I can't let this go Sheena. I'm sorry, I can't. You're my sister and I would never do that to you. He needs to tell me to my face," Ilesha says.

"I agree. He has to explain himself," says Rachel.

"I want to get to the bottom of this too. We should go to his house right now. I'm not waiting. Let's go!" I say.

We all jump into the car with our mean faces on. Ilesha talks about what she's going to do to him and Rachel tries to talk her out of it. I can't wait for his lying ass to backpedal when he sees Ilesha on his doorstep. I think he deserves a nice hard slap from me for this one. The funny thing is that we don't even know if Kevin is home. This is a blind move for us, but it doesn't matter because we are fueled by pure anger and rage. He'll be lucky if he doesn't get cut by Ilesha.

We pull up to his house and see his car is here. We pull in right behind him to block his car in. The first thing Ilesha does is scrape her keys alongside his car. He will not be able to just buff that scratch out. Rachel writes on his windshield the word "liar" in red lipstick. She is so harmless, but she means well. I bang on the door as if the police are about to conduct a raid.

"Who is it?" Kevin asks.

"Don't worry who it is you lying bastard. Just open the damn door!" screams Ilesha.

Rachel asks, "Do you think Kevin will try to hurt us? If he was going to hit the mother of his child, what's stopping him from harming us?"

I seriously doubt Kevin will put his hands on us. My personal belief is that he only attempted to harm me because I spit in his face and threw a cup of water on him. A lot of people feel like spitting in a person's face is the most disrespectful thing you can do to a person. However, I wasn't trying to be disrespectful. I was just angry and I'm even more perturbed now. It's like my anger is a pot of boiling water. It takes time to get me angry, but once a person tries me for too long, my rage boils and takes a while to cool down.

"No, Rachel. I'm not worried about him turning violent. He'll scream, I'm sure, but that's it," I respond.

Ilesha remarks, "It wouldn't be in his best interest to turn violent. There will be no Ike and Tina situations out here today. I don't want to, but if he gets physical, I will be forced to introduce him to Blade. Oh and trust me, I'm not talking about Wesley Snipes."

Ilesha always carries a razor with her. It's like the American Express card because she never leaves home without it. I would hate for her to cut Kevin. That would absolutely be a tragedy. If he goes crazy and attempts to put his hands on any one of us, he will just have to meet Blade. The way I see it, is that it's better him than us. I know if he sees his car keyed, he is going to flip like an Olympic gymnast. I don't see why men are so in love and protective over cars anyway.

"I'm a grown ass man. You don't scream at me like a child," Kevin says as he opens the door.

"I see you opened that door like you were told. Ain't no damn man," says Ilesha.

"Ilesha chill, I got this. Kevin, we didn't come here to cause any trouble, but we did come here to get some answers. You made a very bold and false assertion back at my house about Ilesha. We all want to know why you are making false claims against her," I say.

"Kevin, I never fucked you and you know that's the truth. Tell Sheena what's real, so we can get out of here and let you enjoy the rest of your day," says Ilesha.

Kevin replies, "I can't do that. I'm not in the lying mood. I fucked you. Point, blank, period. Don't be mad at me because I exposed you. You shouldn't be so damn sneaky and freaky."

Rachel stands on the porch shaking her head and covering her face. She is fire red. I can't blame her because I am too. Kevin is so firm in his lying. I ask him again to be truthful, but he is sticking to his nonsense story. Ilesha is not taking this lightly.

"Be a stand-up guy and stop lying on your dick. I know I'm fine as hell, but that doesn't mean you have to bring me into your fantasies. I know why you are lying. I'm beautiful. I get it, but I don't play with people lying on me," Ilesha states.

The two of them go back and forth for a few minutes about who is lying. Both of them are adamant about the other one being full of it. I have been best of friends with Rachel and Ilesha for many years. I've seen them in the best of times and the worst of times. They have never been a tad bit untruthful with me, so I don't see why today is any different.

I state, "Well, this back and forth is getting us nowhere. Just know that you are wrong for this. You think it's cool to try to come between friends, no sisters? I'm not feeling that or you. Let's go girls. I have nothing more to say to him."

"I love the way you ladies stick together. It really warms my heart," Kevin says sarcastically. "I'm not gonna be the only one who gets judged negatively from this situation. I didn't want to do this, but Sheena you pushed me to this point."

"What are you talking about? Do what Kevin, do what?" I question.

"I have video footage of Ilesha and me having sex. I didn't want to show it to you, but you leave me no choice. If you want to see it, I can go get my phone and show you," Kevin replies.

Ilesha chimes in, "Oh, I didn't know you had video footage. You got me..."

I cut Ilesha off without allowing her to finish her sentence and without processing her response. I can't believe Kevin thinks that I really want to see a video of him having sex with somebody. He is out of his mind. The idea of seeing him with another woman is stomach turning. Why would a man take video footage of a sexual encounter? Men are so nasty.

"Kevin, you are a pig! We don't need to see your sex video. We are out of here," I say.

"No, don't leave. I'm gonna prove to you that your friends aren't as devoted as you think they are. Well, at least Ilesha isn't. In my opinion, Rachel isn't so trustworthy either. She was witness to Ilesha talking about my dick. I bet she didn't mention that," Kevin says.

"Kevin, my friendship is unquestionable. And as far as Ilesha's comments that night, I didn't tell Sheena because those were comments made in good humor. Just jokes. There is no point in arguing with a fool," Rachel says.

"Well, I'll prove who the fool is very soon," Kevin retorts.

Kevin jets into the house and comes back with his phone in his hand. He is really running this story all the way to the end. Kevin goes into his phone's menu to find what he's looking for.

"Here it is! The video isn't long, but it's long enough to confirm my story. It's very clear and there isn't any blurriness," Kevin claims.

Kevin shows Rachel and Ilesha the video because I don't want to see it. Rachel cowers in embarrassment while she views the video. Ilesha doesn't wince one bit, but I'm not surprised because she is never flustered. She watches porn by herself and with her boyfriend. She treats this video just like any other sex video she watches.

"Black cat woman top, the facemask, and the black boots. As you can see, I'm clearly fucking Ilesha," says Kevin arrogantly.

Rachel says, "You can't see the woman's face in the video, so I don't know who that is. I'm just being honest."

"Come on! You are just trying to cover for your nasty ass home girl. That's her and you just don't want to admit it. Women stick together even when you know you are dead wrong," Kevin states.

Ilesha says, "He got me. Sheena, I'm sorry, but he got me. I didn't know he had video footage."

"They say a picture is worth a thousand words, so you know a video is worth ten thousand. You were a good fuck. I'm just glad you didn't further insult everyone's intelligence by sticking to your lie. Admit your deceit and move on. That's what Sheena wanted me and Eric to do when she lied to us about who she was pregnant by. Ladies just get over it," Kevin dictates.

I ask, "Ilesha what are you saying?"

"Sheena, you know what I'm saying. Look at the video. I don't want to say it, but it tells everything," says Ilesha.

I look at the video. I am in shock. Kevin is celebrating in the video as he fucks her. In the video, he zooms in on her ass as he smacks it and then videos himself. It's almost like he feels he accomplished something. I've seen all of the video that I need to see. It's confirmed that Kevin is a real piece of shit. I can't believe this. I hand Kevin his phone back and look at Ilesha.

Kevin says, "Now curse her out and call her names like you did me."

"Kevin, you got me," Ilesha voices as she stares at him.

"I know I got you," Kevin promptly replies.

"Yeah, you got me fucked up!" Ilesha replies.

"What do you mean?" asks Kevin.

"You got me fucked up meaning you have me confused with somebody else. That's not me in the video. You slimy bastard!" screams Ilesha.

"Kevin, it was a great try though," I announce.

The girl in the video has the same body features as Ilesha. She appears to be the same height, complexion, and similar curves as Ilesha. The girl in the video never took her mask or top off, but none of that matters. Kevin zoomed in on the girl's booty as he penetrated her and the proof of it not being Ilesha is in that. The woman in the video has a tattoo that reads "Simply Delicious".

Ilesha does have a tattoo on the small of her back, but hers reads "Infatuating". Rachel and I were with her when she got it. I remember that day like it was yesterday. Kevin had sex with an imposter. Why would he have someone fake like Ilesha? Kevin looks confused, so I help him gain some clarity.

"Kevin, look back at the video. Focus on the tattoo," I order.

He pulls the video up and reads the tattoo aloud. Of course, he still has no clue of what the point of that is. Next, I tell Ilesha to pull her shirt up, so he can read that tattoo aloud. His eyes fill up with befuddlement. He looks like he got slapped by an invisible man. We all laugh at him even though this is no laughing matter.

"Pick it up," I order.

"What's that?" Kevin asks.

"Your face is on the ground and you should pick it up," I say.

Kevin explains that he wasn't trying to cause an undue riff between us. He claims that he genuinely thought it was Ilesha that he had sex with. I believe him too. It doesn't make sense for him to have gone this far with his story. I'm livid that he would actually have sex with my friend. You can't trust these men further than you can throw them. Kevin apologizes a million times, but this really doesn't change anything between us. The fact remains that he cheated on me, wanted to fuck my best friend, and attempted to strike me. I'll never be able to erase the image of him fucking another woman out of my brain.

Me and my girls are tight like always. This will go down in the books as one of the most dramatic episodes we've ever been through together. We always have each other's backs. We leave Kevin's house and drive to Ilesha's place. We exposed Kevin as the true selfish asshole he is.

"I couldn't get over the tattoo. I would never have a "Simply Delicious" tattoo because there is nothing simple about my ass. Hell, there isn't anything simple or simply about me at all," Ilesha remarks.

Rachel says, "Girl, you are too much. The girl in the video does have a pretty nice body though."

Ilesha says, "Hmmm, I saw a couple of dimples in her ass. My ass nor body has a wrinkle, dimple, or stretch mark on it. She needs to hit the gym and tighten up."

"Not that I needed to see the video to know it wasn't you, but what did it for me were the girl's shoes. You could see how beat up and dirty they were. There is no way Ilesha would ever have been in those. And they were some no name shoes," I say.

"I'm just glad that this is behind us. I don't like tension and conflict," says Rachel.

"Rachel, there was no conflict or tension amongst us. There was absolutely no part of me that thought Ilesha slept with Kevin," I remark.

Obviously, somebody wanted Kevin to think it was Ilesha he slept with. Kevin ended up playing himself because of it. Who has it in for me? It's undoubtedly someone who's hating on me. Maybe this is Eric's way of getting Kevin out of the picture and keeping me to himself. I know there are a lot of women who are jealous of me. There are plenty of women who would like to break up a happy home. Many women can't find one good man and I had two. There's a lot to consider.

CHAPTER 15
Sheena's Perspective

It's been two weeks since we proved that Kevin didn't have sex with one of my besties. I'm glad it wasn't true. That would have been horrific. The sisterhood would have been broken beyond repair. I know they wouldn't allow a man to infiltrate our unit and that's why I never believed it. If I would have called Ilesha and cursed her out over Kevin's innuendo, we would not be friends right now. I'm so glad I put my trust in the right person.

She would have been insulted by me believing Kevin and by me disrespecting her without hearing her side of the story. In her case, she didn't even have a story to tell. Ilesha was clueless as to what Kevin claimed. I love the way we rode over to Kevin's house and got things settled. The video footage he took proved him wrong. Thank God for video evidence. It felt like we were solving a real life criminal case.

Fortunately, I handled the situation with tact and prudence which is what enabled me to keep my friendship in good standing. Unfortunately, things are not settled with me because I still have no man and I still don't know who Kevin actually slept with. Also, someone went through a tremendous amount of effort to make Kevin think he slept with my best friend. I can't help but wonder who that person is and what their motive was for doing that.

The person essentially attempted to break up my friendship and love life all in one incident. Not knowing who it was doesn't sit well with me. For all I know, the person could still be plotting against me. He or she could be conjuring up a new plan, since their original plan only half worked. I really want to call Eric back because I need to release, but he may be the perpetrator. What is a girl to do?

Ilesha and Rachel both say I should let it go and move on, but it isn't that easy for me. I don't rest well when things are unsettled and up in the air. I seek to bring closure to all things I do. I asked Kevin for as much information as possible, but he was slightly drunk that night and doesn't remember much about it. All he remembers is the girl's tattoo on the small of her back and that's nothing to go on. At least I can say that my romantic involvement with Kevin is over. He cheated on me and threatened me physically, so we can only deal when it's pertaining to our son. The way he's treated me should negate him from any contact with me, but I won't do that to my son.

Even though I won't prevent him from seeing Devin, he won't be allowed in my house. I'm going to have all of the locks changed. He can come to the front porch or I'll just drop Devin off at his house or maybe we'll just meet somewhere neutral. Honestly, I don't want him near me. He should really seek anger management counseling. I hope my son doesn't inherit that mean streak that Kevin has. That would be depressing.

I need to focus on what I'm doing for myself. I've been entertaining a couple of men who have asked me out. It's nothing serious with them, but it helps occupy my time. I'm not willing to sit home and do nothing all of the time. Hell, I need some attention from the opposite sex. I can't and won't keep interrupting my girls' lives. I'm at In the Mix meeting Sage for lunch. He's been trying to woo me lately. He's made it clear that he's grown a lot since we were a couple.

I want to give him my goods like nobody's business, but it's just too soon. I need to know for sure that he's not the same little boy from years ago. If he has learned how to keep his dick in his pants, he's a great candidate for a relationship. We have a lot in common. For example, we are both college educated, we both own our own businesses, and we both are attractive. The similarities are endless. I also like that he doesn't have children. I know I have kids, but that doesn't mean I want a man with kids too. My girls call me a hypocrite, but it doesn't bother me one bit. I really don't have time for baby momma drama. Sage approaches me.

"Sheena, you look stunning. I apologize for keeping you waiting. I hope it wasn't too long," Sage comments.

I reply, "Thank you! No, it wasn't long at all."

Sage states, "I saw you come in, but I was stuck on the phone with one of my vendors. He's trying to switch the delivery times for some of his products and that's not going to work for me. I mean we signed off on the commitment dates and times weeks ago."

"I understand. Unfortunately, I've been there too many times. You know people will tell you anything and everything you want to hear on the front end to get your business and then try to switch things up on the back end," I reply.

Sage states, "Isn't that the truth and it really bothers me, but I guess it's a drawback of running a business."

"It sure is. I'm sure you got the situation taken care of," I say.

"That's without question. I told him that I'll find a new vendor if he can't fulfill the contract he signed and will sue him for breach of contract. I always keep a backup just in case. He changed his tune once I said that," Sage reports.

"I heard that. You can't play when it comes to business," I articulate.

"Right, right, but enough about work. How are things with you?" Sage asks.

We share great conversation like we always do. He is a master of using the right words to lock you into what he's talking about. Sage knows when to throw a joke at me and when to let me dominate the conversation. I see why the girls who patronize the club love him so much. Honestly, everybody loves Sage. In the Mix would not be the success that it is without him. I still find it hard to believe that he got shot in his office some years back.

He never elaborates on what happened the day he got shot or what the reason was. He normally downplays it and skips over anything detailed. Sage wants to show me some ideas he has for a potential renovation to the club. He goes and gets his iPad from his office and returns to the table. He sits right beside me in the booth, so he can show me the pictures.

He knows that I have an eye for all things that look good. It doesn't matter if it's interior decor, clothing, or men because I'm on point in all areas. Trust me; I have great fashion taste pumping through my veins. We look at countless images and converse about what fits and why.

We share many laughs while we talk.

My smile is soon turned into a frown when I look over at the door. To my dismay, Kevin walks into the lounge. He doesn't appear to be happy either and begins to walk toward our table. His facial expressions and body language tell me that this may not be a pleasant encounter. I need to alert Sage just in case Kevin decides to attack him.

"Sage, the guy with the black sweatpants and black shirt is the father of my child. We aren't together, but he looks angry and I'm not sure what he'll do. Just be careful when he gets over here," I report.

Kevin arrives at our booth and stands there staring at me, but doesn't say a word. I hope he isn't waiting for me to say anything because I don't have anything to say to him. He can miss me with his whining and hurt feelings. He let his insecurities ruin a happy home and for that I'll never forgive him. That was an emotional incident and he only thought of himself.

"You seem to be mighty friendly in here today. Nice and cozy like I don't exist," says Kevin.

"I am enjoying myself if that's what you mean. I hope you didn't come here to spoil my time and cause trouble," I reply.

Kevin asks, "Are you gonna act like you didn't get any of my phone calls? Where the hell is my son?"

I like that Sage hasn't intervened. He's minding his business and allowing me to handle mine. If Sage jumps into this, it's not going to be a happy ending. Sage has seen me handle myself in many situations, so he knows that I'm adept. Sage continues to look at the pictures on his iPad. Many women would want him to take over, but I'm a big girl and I can handle this little riff.

"Kevin, I'm gonna need you to lower your voice and remove the aggression from it too. Feel free to have a seat and we can discuss matters," I calmly reply.

Kevin has a seat at the table and Sage excuses himself. Sage claims that he has some business to tend to, but I know it isn't true. He just wants us have our privacy while we talk. I don't blame him because I don't like to be in the middle of other people's affairs.

"Where is my son and why are you spending so much time down here?" Kevin asks.

"You know where your son is. I told you that my mom and aunt were taking the boys to Disneyland. I don't know why you carry yourself the way you do. It kinda sickens me," I say.

"How exactly am I acting? How would you act if I didn't return your calls and you hadn't seen your son in far too long?" Kevin asks.

I promptly reply, "I think you're acting like a bitch. You are way too emotional right now. And as for not seeing my son, I would miss him, but as long as I knew he's in good hands, I wouldn't trip about it."

"Oh, so I'm a bitch now? A man shows some concern over his son and he's a bitch?" Kevin asks in an extremely loud voice as he rises from the table and knocks over the salt and pepper shakers.

"I never said you are a bitch. I'm saying you are acting like one. Those are two different things," I state.

Kevin becomes infuriated by my comments. I know my lack of emotional investment in this feud is making him even more upset. Kevin is cursing and making a big scene over nothing. I don't understand men sometimes. If he couldn't handle my answer to his question, why even ask it? He set himself up to get his feelings hurt.

Sage hears what's going on and inspects the situation. It's such a scene that all of the waiters, waitresses, and customers are all staring at us. I hate that this is happening. I'm not one who condones or participates in public drama. It doesn't have to be this way. It could have been handled discreetly.

Sage questions, "Is everything okay over here?"

Kevin responds, "My man, no it's not okay over here. You are in here making lovie dovie with my lady and I don't appreciate it one damn bit."

I don't allow Sage an opportunity to answer because what Kevin is saying is false.

I say, "I am not your lady, so stop telling people that. Let me find out that the only reason you came up here is to bother me about being up here. I know you're stalking me."

Kevin says, "I do what the hell I want to do. If I wanna check up on you, I will."

Sage chimes in, "Sir, at my establishment people follow the rules I set forth. You are behaving with hostility and with no regard for my patrons. I need you to leave the premises NOW or you'll be removed NOW."

Sage isn't a fighter, but Kevin surely is. I hope this doesn't get physical because I think Sage may get beat down. I'd hate to see them fight, but I won't hesitate to take my phone out and record the entire altercation. I have men all over the place fighting over me. I'm tickled over the way Sage got politically correct on Kevin. His flow and oratory skills got me slightly moist. A strong man is such a turn on for me. Ilesha will be jealous and Rachel will give a Dr. King speech against violence.

"I know you don't intend to remove me by yourself," Kevin says as he turns to Sage in a battle stance.

"You'll either walk out on your own or I'll escort you out on my own. The choice is yours," Sage says.

I guess Kevin wasn't taking a chance of getting beat up by Sage because he throws a series of punches at Sage with the speed of fan blades spinning on high. What shocks me even more is the way Sage handles them. He ducks, dips, and dodges all of the blows Kevin's throwing. Sage looks like he is related to Bruce Lee. Eventually, Kevin goes rushing in at Sage to grab his legs in an attempt to slam him.

I have my camera rolling and I'm not missing any of the action. Sage knees Kevin in the face as he rushes in. Kevin falls to the floor and Sage dives on him and puts him in the choke hold. Kevin squirms around trying to get out of the hold, but can't get free. Kevin even tries scratching Sage's face, but it's to no avail.

"Calm down and I'll let you go. Nod your head if you're calm," Sage orders.

Kevin nods his head, so Sage lets him go and stands up. Kevin is livid and I'm sure if he had a weapon on him, he'd surely use it on Sage. Everyone in the establishment is screaming and hollering. Many people are shouting in support of Sage's efforts while others are yelling in disapproval of Kevin's behavior.

"My friend, it's time for you to go. Looks like your phone is on the floor over there. I need you to grab it and leave," Sage says.

Kevin replies with a very harsh, "Fuck you!"

Kevin apparently has not had enough because he squares off with Sage again.

I scream, "Kevin, please stop! You're making a spectacle of yourself!"

He ignores my plea. Sage puts his hands up

in a defensive stance and they begin boxing again. Kevin throws one wild punch at Sage, but it's like someone told Sage it was coming an hour before Kevin threw it because Sage side steps the punch and hits Kevin with a crushing blow to his throat. The punch drops Kevin instantaneously. Sage and another employee drag Kevin out of the club. One of the waitresses runs over and asks Sage what to do.

"Sage, do you want me to call the cops?" the waitress asks.

"No, it's not necessary. We have it under control," Sage replies.

I'm glad Sage doesn't want to call the authorities, because the last thing I need is for Kevin to get arrested. He's a man from corporate America for God's sake. If he were to get arrested, that could compromise his career. I can't have my son's father be unemployed. Where would that leave Devin? They carry Kevin to the car and I follow. He tries to talk to me before he pulls away, but I don't stick around.

CHAPTER 16
Sheena's Perspective

I go back inside to chat with Sage before I leave. Only in my life. My life used to be so simple. All of that changed when I started double dealing. The funny thing is that I don't know which life I like better. The simple life has its perks, but so does a life filled with drama. A simple life allows you to sit back and relax. For the most part, you can predict what's going to happen from day to day. A drama filled life is fun because it's so unpredictable. The suspense keeps me on the edge of my seat and eager to see what's to come. Unfortunately, it can easily become a headache and stressful.

I haven't had guys fight over me like this since high school. Now it seems like they're fighting over me regularly. What would I be doing if all of this wasn't happening? I apologize to Sage for the disruption at his place. He assures me that it's okay. I leave In the Mix and call Ilesha because I'm heading her way. I need to tell her what I've seen and show her the video. I'm sure she'll be amazed.

I jump out of my car and run in Ilesha's house. I don't know if I even put the car in park. I'm just eager to let her know what's going on.

"Girl, you won't believe the fight I saw today. It was crazy and I got the entire thing on video. I was right on top of it," I report.

"Who was fighting and where were you at?" Ilesha asks.

I reply proudly, "It was Sage and Kevin. They fought at In the Mix right in the dining area!"

"Girl, you had them fighting over you too? What in the hell happened? You know I want all the details," Ilesha says.

I give her all the details of what happened. After I narrate what happened, I show her the video in its entirety. We watch the video as if it's a Steven Segal action flick. We laugh all the way through. I tell her to ride back to In the Mix, so I can show her where it all went down.

While we're riding to the lounge, Ilesha watches the video several more times. She even wants to post the fight online for all to see. I don't allow her to do so because I don't want Kevin to suffer that much public embarrassment. People are very cruel and will never let him live that down. Additionally, he is a career man and doesn't need that negative attention.

We walk in and go to the booth where Sage beat him down. The waitress comes over and asks us for our order.

"We would like two Miamis," I say.

The waitress gives us a befuddled look. I can tell she doesn't have the slightest idea of what that is. I'm not surprised because it's a drink that started in my hometown of Linden, New Jersey. I tell her what to put in the drink and she walks away.

"Girl, I haven't had a Miami since I got drunk off them in Nuno's Pavilion in Linden. The Coconut Cîroc mixed with pineapple juice and a splash of cranberry had me on my ass," Ilesha reports.

"Hell, I know what you mean because I was right there with you. If Rachel wasn't the designated driver that night, we would have never gotten home. That Miami makes you feel like you are on South Beach," I reply.

"I love that girl to death. Why isn't she here anyway?" asks Ilesha.

"I didn't invite her because she doesn't need to be a part of what may happen in here. I may need to get ratchet in a minute and I don't need anybody trying to talk me out of it. I'm not with the voice of reason right now. I just want to turn up if I need to and I know you have my back," I reply.

Ilesha replies, "I thought it was strange that you wanted me to come down here right after you left, but I wanted to get out of the house, so it didn't matter to me. You know I got your back on whatever it is, but bring me up to speed."

"Look around and tell me what you see," I reply.

"Okay, I see tables, chairs, the bar, and people," Ilesha comments.

I perk up and say, "Exactly! You see women. Light skinned women. Now look at them a bit closer."

Ilesha begins to examine every woman in the lounge. I wait patiently for her eyes to zero in on what I saw after the brawl. I notice Ilesha getting frustrated because she hasn't seen what I have just yet.

"I give up. Girl, just tell me because my eyes are starting to hurt from all this glaring," Ilesha orders.

"Just watch the girl cleaning those tables by the DJ booth. You'll see what I'm talking about very soon," I say.

Ilesha studies the girl I directed her to. Her eyes get huge as she makes the connection I hoped she would.

Ilesha looks over at me and says, "Simply Delicious! That bitch!"

"Now you know how I feel. I saw her tattoo at the end of the fight when they were carrying Kevin out to his car. My first instinct was to yank her ass, but I thought better of it," I say.

"Well, I'm glad you thought better of it, because now that means I get to yank her ass. She is gonna wish she never impersonated me," Ilesha says.

Ilesha jumps up from the table. I think she is going to confront the girl right here, so I stop her. I don't want to make another scene here at the club. I know if we whoop her ass, we'll never get all the information we want from her. I can't help but to think how fortuitous it is that Kevin made the video of him hitting her from the back.

"Don't go over there and bother her," I say.

"Relax, I'm not going over to her. I have on a pair of thirteen hundred dollar red bottoms and I'm not messing them up for her," Ilesha reports.

"Good girl. I never know with you. You're always ready no matter what," I convey.

"You know I'm always ready to throw down. I have my gym bag in the car, so I'm going to get it. I'm gonna put on my riot gear and then I'm gonna whoop her ass," replies Ilesha.

I say, "Girl, go get your bag and then we'll talk."

Ilesha comes back in with her gym bag and her attitude on ten. She isn't feeling good about the female who impersonated her. I tell her to listen to the plan I have and not to approach the girl just yet. We have to wait for the right opportunity. If we swing on her now, there's no way we'll get to the bottom of this.

We must be strategic and meticulous in all things that we do. That's how a true woman makes moves. If we start a commotion, we probably will have the police arresting us. I'm not "bout that life". I give Ilesha the details of the plan. She goes and changes into her workout clothes just in case it gets violent.

When Ilesha comes back to the table, we put the plan into action. Ilesha and I walk into the restroom. A minute after we go into the bathroom, Ilesha runs back into the bar area and summons the waitress with the "Simply Delicious" tattoo.

"Excuse me, but my friend needs some assistance in the restroom. She's fallen and can't get up," Ilesha says.

The waitress rushes into the bathroom with Ilesha following her on her heels. As soon as they enter the bathroom, I close the door shut and block it with the trashcan. We begin to interrogate the female. We corner the girl up against the mirror along the wall.

"What's going on here?" she asks.

"We just have a few questions to ask you and want you to be honest and straight forward with us," I say.

"First of all, I don't know you and get the hell off of me before I get upset. You two don't know who I am," she states aggressively.

She begins to squirm in an attempt to get away, so Ilesha slaps her and I grab her arms. I inform her that the last thing we want to do is have a fight in the bathroom and that we just need to talk to her. She is still a little agitated, but calms down a bit after I bang her head against the mirror.

"I know you fucked my man after the Halloween party. I'm not tripping off that because like you said before I don't know you. I just wanna know what all the extra stuff was about," I say.

"Yeah, you acting like other people, so you can get some dick. I mean you're a cute girl, so I don't understand why you pretended to be me. That isn't right," Ilesha chimes in.

"You caused a lot of confusion and drama that didn't have to be," I say.

"Yeah, we had sex. It was a one night stand and we haven't communicated since, but let us be clear, I didn't pretend to be anyone," the waitress says.

"So what was the deal with the cat suit?" Ilesha asks.

"Yeah, and why would Kevin think you were Ilesha?" I ask.

"It was just a fuck. I'm young and he was looking good, so I went to his house after a couple of drinks. We didn't even talk. I walked through the door, zipped his pants down, and went to work on him," the waitress reports.

"That doesn't make any sense. You couldn't show up at his house without having talked to him and your costume was no accident," I say.

"Listen, Sage is the one who told me that the guy in the Shaft costume was interested. Sage told me that he was into role playing, so I just went along with everything. I'm in school and only work here part-time. I don't have money for a leather cat suit. Sage gave me that too," says the waitress.

"Okay, Sage bought the cat suit. We get that, but tell us about the red thong you left behind with my initial on it," Ilesha challenges.

I chime in, "Yeah, your name tag says Leslie, so it doesn't make sense that your thong would have the letter 'I' on it. You were definitely trying to be Ilesha."

"Slow down girls. Yes, my name is Leslie, but my line name is Instantaneous. I don't think I need to share all of my business with you, but I'm trying to help you out. The thong was a gift that my soror gave to the bridal party when she got married. We all got monogrammed thongs, among other things. And the thong is not red, it's crimson. Thank you very much," Leslie states.

I'm at a loss for words. I never saw this conversation going this way. Sage is the person behind all of this. What an asshole! I should have known that he'd be responsible for this drama behind my back. He is always brewing up something. If I didn't know any better, I'd think he's responsible for hurricanes and tornadoes.

RYAN HODGE

"Girl, I'm so sorry. I had no idea he even had a girlfriend. If I would have known, I never would have fucked him. I was misled," Leslie orates.

The conversation goes from hostile to almost sisterly. We apologize for coming at the waitress with so much force. She accepts our apology and we let her get back to work. We ask her not to let Sage know about the revelations we've made today. She agrees not to make him abreast of our discussion. She is upset with Sage too because he used her for his sneaky plan. He put her in the middle of a situation that she shouldn't have anything to do with.

"Damn girl, that's so fucked up," comments Ilesha.

"I know right. Sage has gone too far this time. He tried to burn our friendship and burned my relationship with Kevin," I utter.

"Yeah, that too. I was saying that it's fucked up because I really wanted to whoop her ass," Ilesha replies.

"Girl, you know that you are nothing, but crazy!" I mention as I laugh.

"She is clearly not as sexy as I am. Her titties are kinda saggy to be so young. When we were young like that, everything on our bodies was tight and perky. No stretch marks or meat rolls anywhere in sight," says Ilesha.

"Hell, it's still like that on my body now and that's after delivering a set of twins. I didn't like

186

the weight I gained while I was carrying, but it happened and I got it all off of me," I remark.

"I think these girls are eating too many snacks. Drake's Tasty Cakes and Little Debbie are whooping these young girl's asses. Look like they drink from the fountain of soda too," jokes Ilesha.

I'm glad she threw a joke in there. It really lightened the mood. My mind is all out of whack again. It's like a race car track with cars traveling against the flow of traffic. We leave In the Mix and drive back to Ilesha's house. I drop her off and go back to my place. I have a headache and need to relax my mind. I feel a long hot bath and a chilled glass of wine in my near future.

CHAPTER 17
Sheena's Perspective

The next day we bring Rachel up to speed on what happened at In the Mix. She is astonished to hear that Sage and Kevin had a fight. Rachel is even more shocked to hear that Sage won the fight so convincingly. I have to admit that I was surprised too. Kevin beat Eric down with no problem and is always so aggressive, so I thought he'd easily dispatch Sage. Sage never talks about fighting and makes it seem as if he can't fight. Rachel is disappointed that we didn't allow her to be a part of the drama.

"I could have added some valuable insight to helping you through a troubling time," Rachel states.

Ilesha states, "The only insight you would've added would have been to not confront the waitress. You also would've started crying and reciting some words from Dr. King. We shall overcome some day."

We start cracking up laughing. Rachel laughs too because she knows we are right. She'd never let us go through with confronting that girl.

"Just because I don't like to fight, doesn't mean I wouldn't have supported my sisters in their time of need. I can be ratchet if I need to be," Rachel claims.

"Bitch please! If you're ratchet, that means I'm a virgin. We all know that I'm many great fucks away from being a virgin," Ilesha says.

"Rachel, you are a lot of things, but ratchet isn't one of them. Sorry dear, but you're just a sweetheart. It just is what it is," I reply.

I show Rachel the video of Sage and Kevin's fight. She covers her eyes and mouth as she watches every blow of the scuffle. She can barely stand to watch the fight on video, but claims to be ratchet. She wants to be supportive of us, so she sometimes steps out of her comfort zone. We love her for her willingness to help, but you have to know who to call when you need certain things. My dear Rachel is not the one to call during a situation that may get physical. Ilesha, on the other hand, is perfectly suited for arguing and fighting.

"Girl, I don't know why we're still here talking. It's time to take action. Retaliation is on my mind," Ilesha says as she pounds her fist into her hand.

I say, "I'm definitely looking for revenge. Sage tried to break us up. He knows how much I love my girls."

"Okay, it's settled. We are going to Sage's house now and whoop his ass. I don't care because I will fight a man. I'm going for his car first and then I'll put my hands on him," says Ilesha.

"Honey, I know you're mad, but you shouldn't bring harm to Sage. He'll have to answer to his maker one day. I think we should have a conference with him to determine why he did what he did," replies Rachel.

"A conference? What the hell we gonna do with a conference? You want us to talk him to death?" Ilesha asks.

"No, but violence begets more violence. We should seek to understand and then heal the man," Rachel declares.

"See, that's that bullshit I'm talking about," Ilesha replies.

"Rachel, I hear where you are coming from, but that's a bit much. Sage has to pay for his deceitful ways. He has to feel my wrath for his deception," I report.

Ilesha chimes in, "Thank you! I knew you'd see it my way. Take my razor. I have another one in the car. Let's go and find him now. I'm ready!"

I reply, "Ilesha, he has to be held accountable for his actions. I'm the first to admit it, but not quite the way you think."

Rachel asks, "What do you have in mind? If you don't want violence brought to Sage and you don't want to talk, what do you want to happen?"

I tell the girls that I have the perfect payback for his little conniving self. I'm all about teaching men lessons. I gave Sage a pass back in the day for not being sensitive to my feelings, but now being kind is out of the question. Sage takes kindness for weakness and I'm done playing the victim.

Sage will regret doing this. Sage intentionally ruined my relationship with Kevin and indirectly caused a conflict with Eric, so it's his turn to have to deal with drama. Sage's days of smooth sailing are almost over because I'm bringing the storm to him.

"What's the plan? Can I be in on it?" Rachel asks.

"I don't know because you know you have a kind heart. You might regret it halfway through the plan," I reply.

"Girl, you know I have your back. If you need me, I'm here undoubtedly. Just let me know," Rachel replies.

I respond, "I will."

Ilesha blurts out, "Hell, I know I'm doing something to help out, since Sage brought me into all of this. His ass is mine."

"Okay, it's settled. We'll teach him a lesson together just like we did Eric and Kevin when this all started," I explain.

I tell my girls the plan and their respective roles. They agree to their duties. We are excited about the possibility of how well this plot is going to work out. It's time to put operation "Get Back" into effect.

Rachel and Ilesha head over to In the Mix. I'm sure Sage is there because today is one of his delivery days. He likes to make sure all of his orders are filled the way they are supposed to be. Sage is a slight control freak, so I have to use that to my advantage.

Rachel and Ilesha walk into In the Mix and take a seat at our normal booth. Moments later Sage approaches their table just like we planned. The ladies are outraged from Sage's attempt to bring conflict to our sisterhood, but they have to control their feelings for now. If Sage senses any tension between them, he'll become defensive and suspicious.

"Hello ladies," Sage says.

Rachel replies, "Hi, Sage. How are you?"

Sage states, "I'm well. No complaints here."

Ilesha, staying true to form states, "You two are so formal. It's killing me. Hi Sage works for me. That's all your ass is getting."

Sage laughs at Ilesha's response. That's her normal, so Sage doesn't think much of it.

"I wouldn't expect anything other than that from you Ilesha. I know I'm not your most favorite person in the world these days," says

Sage.

"Hell, you know I never did like what you did to Sheena back in the day, but she's past it, so I guess I can get past it too," replies Ilesha.

"That's cool. I was young and full of myself and full of games, but I'm a new man now. Have to grow up at some point. Kids play games, but men handle business," Sage narrates.

Sage's response nauseates Rachel and Ilesha because he is acting like he's so righteous and above the game playing now, but in reality he's just as sneaky and underhanded as he's always been. My girls are seasoned veterans, so they don't lose form. They stay in character and complete their mission.

Rachel states, "I have to say that from what I've seen from you lately, you are more mature these days. Maturity looks good on you and I'm not the only one who's noticing."

"Thanks. I now know the error of my ways, so I changed my ways. I'm on to bigger and better things. Grown man moves," Sage explains.

He really possesses the gift of gab. If they didn't know him, they would be thoroughly convinced that he had a great reformation. He isn't a changed man at all.

"We all had some growing to do back then, including myself," says Ilesha.

"Rachel, you said you weren't the only one who noticed my change. Who else has?" asks Sage.

Ilesha answers, "Nobody else has. Rachel was just telling a little too much of the business. Don't worry about it."

"Is that the truth Rachel?" Sage questions.

"All I'll say is that Sheena has been speaking very highly of you lately and that you should keep doing whatever it is that you're doing. By the way, she is single right now," Rachel reports.

"It's great to know that my efforts are not being done in vain. You just made my day. Oh, don't worry; I'll be sure to keep my efforts sustained. I'm definitely trying to get back in there with her," Sage replies.

"You should ask her out. You may have a good night with a happy ending. You never know, but it's worth a try," states Rachel.

My girls - my sisters have set the trap ever so smoothly. They should be up for academy awards. Sage really fell for the fraudulent performance. He's not as perceptive as I gave him credit to be, but he is going up against me, so I should expect him to be outwitted. He is so worried about sexing me that he can't see what's really brewing.

Rachel and Ilesha leave In the Mix shortly after they set the bait. I appreciate their help like always. Without them, I'd be a sunken ship at the bottom of the ocean. Just as I expect, the plan works to perfection. Sage is calling me now. He didn't even wait a day to dial me up. I put on my sweet and energetic voice. I have to play like I'm really happy to hear from him.

"Hey, I was just thinking about you," I say after I answer the phone.

"I was thinking about you too, so I figured I'd give you a call. I needed to hear your warm and inviting voice. You've made my day," Sage says.

"That's sweet. Thank you," I say.

Sage asks, "What were you thinking about? Were you thinking about how I used to make your body quiver?"

"I know you wanna know what I was thinking about, but I'm not telling you. You'll just have to wonder," I say jokingly.

"I really do want to know, but it's cool. You have the tight mouth right now, but you know a closed mouth doesn't get fed. Open up, so I can feed your soul," Sage retorts.

I know I have him right where I want him. This game of cat and mouse is intriguing to Sage. He lives for this battle-of-the-wits type of conversation. He always wants to see if he can extract the information he wants out of you without you knowing it. He wants to feed my soul and I'll feed his ego.

"What were you thinking about? Was it juicy and steamy?" I ask.

"No, it wasn't steamy, but thinking of you is always refreshing," Sage replies.

I ask, "Are you trying to make me blush?"

He thinks he has me now. Only if he knew

what was really going on. I won't tell him and will continue to sell the dream.

"Miss, you are someone special and I know I dropped the ball with my movements, but I want you to know that I can fix this. I will make things right because you are my light. You are my vision," Sage eloquently states.

"I don't see how you can fix this. I really don't," I say.

I really don't want to invite him over, so I'll let him get to that. I'll draw him in with a quick comment.

"Just give me a moment of your time for me to explain myself and I'm sure you'll understand," Sage reports.

"Well, my phone is about to die, so it won't be right now. Maybe next week or something we'll chat again," I reply.

I know Sage wants to get whatever is on his chest off, so next week is totally out of the question. He is one who likes to finalize things. It would kill him to go all week. For him, it would be like toting a ton of bricks.

Sage states, "No, next week is an eternity from now. If you're going to be home, I don't have a problem stopping by now."

It really pays to know how people think. He is putting himself right where I want him to be. I definitely want him over here, but not right now.

"I have some things to do right now, so you can't come now. Come by later today. I'll call or text when it's okay for you to come by," I explain.

Sage states, "Don't make me wait too long, but I'll be ready when you call."

"You better be. It may be in your best interest to bring a change of clothes," I say.

"Is that right?" Sage asks.

"That's what I said, but it really depends on how you act when you arrive. You need to be on point," I say.

"On point with what?" Sage asks.

"Don't worry about it. Just be ready when I call," I say.

"Okay, I will," Sage says.

I hang up with Sage and call Kevin. I tell Kevin that we need to talk face to face. He agrees to my suggestion. I want to get out the house, so I go to Kevin's house instead of him coming to mine. I put on a tight black dress and some heels to wear to Kevin's house. I know he'll swear that I'm going out and that will enrage him.

I need him to be an emotional wreck. I will be able to manipulate him more effectively if he's vulnerable. In my opinion, men are clay and I am the hands that shape them. I drive to Kevin's house and text him to open the door. I walk inside and we greet each other.

Kevin says, "I'll be honest, I never expected to see you here at my house again."

I respond sternly, "After that stunt you

pulled, I really shouldn't be here, but we do have a son together, so I'll at least be cordial for his sake."

"I understand and do appreciate it. By the way, you look stunning in your little black dress," Kevin remarks.

I say, "Keep your flattery. I don't need it right now. I can't believe you really attempted to sleep with my best friend."

"I'm sorry for that. My feelings were all over the place and I lost my better judgment for a minute. I have my clarity back and hope we can get past this," states Kevin.

"Hmmm, you don't know what it'll take to make it up to me. Your efforts will have to be herculean to say the least," I say.

"I'm up to the challenge because I know I fucked up. I'll do whatever it takes," Kevin says.

"I'm gonna hold you to that," I say.

"Can you stay for dinner?" Kevin asks.

"Oh no. I have plans with Sage later, so I won't be available," I report.

I spill the beans about hanging with Sage to piss Kevin off. I know he loathes Sage and despises me hanging with him even more. Sage beating him up killed any chance of a friendly relationship between them. I know he'll have a negative comment about me meeting up with Sage later.

"I guess he's the reason why you have on that tight black dress. You don't need to be around him. He doesn't mean you any good," Kevin says.

"Don't tell me who to consort with. You obviously thought he was cool enough to tell your business to," I respond.

"What do you mean by that?" Kevin says.

I respond, "You told him that you were interested in Ilesha and he used that information against you. Sage is the one who sent the girl you thought was Ilesha to your house. He set up the entire thing to separate me from you and me from Ilesha."

"You have to be joking. I was a little tipsy that night and was off my "A" game. That's why he was feeding me drinks. He clearly knew I had dealings with you. He even volunteered to hook me up with Ilesha," Kevin narrates.

"Yes, he used you to get to me and you unwittingly helped him," I say.

"I'm gonna go upside his head. He caught me at my worst the other day at In the Mix, but he won't again. I'll break his ribs this time," Kevin says.

I say, "Relax. He'll beat your ass again for sure. Think bigger and outside the box. If you wanna get him back listen to me and vengeance will be yours."

"What do you have in mind?" Kevin asks.

I tell Kevin the plan and that he needs to meet me at my house later this evening. I need all hands on deck to make this work. Kevin is more than willing to help me out because he dislikes Sage more than he dislikes Eric. My poor baby Eric. I've been giving him the cold shoulder lately. I plan to make things right with him when I settle all of this drama.

CHAPTER 18
Sheena's Perspective

Once I have Kevin on board with my scheme, I call Sage to tell him to come over to my place at eight o'clock sharp. I tell Kevin to come over at seven thirty. I know Sage will be his usual ten minutes early, so I have Kevin come by well before Sage.

I hear my doorbell ringing promptly at seven thirty. I go downstairs and let Kevin in the house. Kevin will be upstairs and out of sight when Sage arrives.

"You turned your phone off and parked your car around the corner like I told you to?" I ask.

"Yeah, Sheena. I followed your instructions to the letter. My end is covered. I still don't see how you're gonna pull this off, but I know you are competent," Kevin replies.

Kevin and I talk for a few more minutes and

then the doorbell rings again. This time it's Sage. Kevin scurries up the stairs and relaxes in my guest bedroom to avoid being detected by Sage. I hope he doesn't make any noise and blow the plan before I can make this payback happen.

I open the door for Sage and we have a seat in the living room. He's looking and smelling great as always. There is nothing new about that. I want to slap his face off, but I have to keep my composure. Physical harm will not bother him. The only thing he cares about is his dick and his money. I can't deny the fact that his package is lovely, but that's irrelevant now.

"Would you like a drink?" I ask.

"Yes, you know my drink of choice. No need for me to tell you. Just fix it because you know how I like it," Sage replies.

"Are you being sexual?" I ask.

Sage responds, "Maybe. Maybe not."

I fix Sage and myself a drink. We sit in the living room while we enjoy our adult beverages. Sage is eyeballing me as if I'm a meal and he's starving to death. I know he wants me and my goods. He thinks he's going to get some, but it's not happening. Time to play cat and mouse.

"You wanted to talk to me? About what?" I ask.

Sage replies, "Yes, I understand that you are single again and I want you to know that I want to fill your vacancy. I'm the perfect man for the job."

I reply, "Obviously, someone has been spreading my business. Either that or you're a stalker. I'd bet it's a little of both."

Sage says, "I just pay attention to the things and people who matter to me the most."

I'll let Sage think he is in control of the situation, but I'm clearly running the show. All I'll do is throw him a few easy questions about us and he'll swear he's in the driver's seat. I'll essentially be stroking his ego and at the same time I'll be concealing my true intentions.

"Is that right? You pay attention to the people who matter the most? Am I supposedly one of the people who fall on that list?" I ask.

"That's not even a question. I wouldn't be here in front of you now if you weren't on the list. You're on the top of the list. In fact, you're the only one on my list. These other girls are just that – girls. They can't hold a candle to you or even be mentioned in the same breath as you," Sage comments.

"Prove it Mr. Bigshot," I say.

Sage takes everything as a challenge, so he won't back down. He always has something to prove.

Sage says, "I'll buy you whatever you want or take you wherever you want to go. Just pick the place. We can shop on Rodeo Drive or travel overseas."

"Sorry Sage. That's too easy of a task for you. Shopping and traveling only require money

RYAN HODGE

being spent and we both know you have no problem with making or spending money. You'll spend your money on anyone," I say.

"Well I tried, so I don't know what else to tell you. Every king needs a queen to make his empire complete and I want you to be my queen. I guess what I'm saying is that I want to be your man. You know you mean the world to me," Sage replies.

I state, "If I mean anything to you, you will be able to answer these simple questions pertaining to me and to us. This should be easy, since you claim I mean so much to you."

"This will be a cake walk, but I don't see the point," Sage says.

I reply, "Your responses will determine if you go to my bedroom tonight or to yours. This could determine our future together."

"I guess this is serious. Well, I'm ready for whatever you throw at me. I've never failed a test in my life, so I don't expect this test to be any different from the others," Sage replies confidently.

I ask, "What's my middle name?"

"If you're going to ask me easy questions like that, we can skip this and head straight upstairs. You can be honest with me and tell me you want some loving tonight," Sage says.

"I do want you upstairs, but you have to earn it. It's not gonna be simple for you," I say.

Sage asks, "What else you got? Do you have

204

any difficult questions?"

"You ready for the real questions? Who starred in the first movie we ever saw together? I got you this time, didn't I? Do you wanna use your phone?" I ask.

"No, I don't need a crutch. You are quite comical. I really don't understand the point of this charade. We can just head to your room and start a fire. Burn those sheets up," Sage replies.

I say, "You only say that because you don't know the correct answer."

"Ashley Judd is the answer. Thank you very much. I'm definitely going upstairs tonight," Sage answers.

I ask Sage a bunch of other easy questions that he easily answers. I make them seem difficult, but I know they aren't. He thinks he has really gotten the upper hand tonight, but he is exactly where I want him to be.

"Okay, okay. Enough of the questions. You clearly know a lot about me. Let's go upstairs and see what else you remember about what I like," I say.

Sage's face lights up upon receiving my suggestion. I know he's been wanting some of me ever since I let him eat me out in his office. His dick was rock hard that night and I'm sure it will be long and strong again tonight. I hope it is. His sex game is so good that you'll think he invented sex.

I grab the wine and Sage grabs the glasses.

He walks up the stairs behind me caressing my ass with his free hand and nibbling on my neck. I'm slightly turned on and feel my palace of pleasure getting wet. I can't let him see that I want him badly. I have to stay focused.

We sit on the bed and sip the wine. Sage pulls out his phone and goes to his playlist. The first song that plays is a song Sage wrote for me when we were in undergrad. I haven't heard that song in forever. He extends his hand and I grab it. We dance slowly and passionately to the song.

I feel Sage's dick gently poking through his pants. It feels heavenly up against me. I haven't had any sexual healing in far too long. I need another drink. This wine is not strong enough.

"Sage, can you get me the Patrón from downstairs?" I ask.

"Your wish is my command," says Sage.

I walk into the bathroom and check myself out in the mirror. I'm certainly looking good as hell. By the time I walk back into the room, Sage is back upstairs. I need to hurry up because I know Kevin is getting restless in the other room.

"Sage, you look tense. Your face is real tight. Almost like you have a great deal of pressure that needs to be released. I can help you with that," I say.

I walk over to him and yank him by his belt buckle. He doesn't resist. I unbuckle his belt, unbutton his pants, and zip down his zipper. I pull his pants and underwear down. His dick is exposed. I stop for a moment and look him in the eyes while I fondle his dick until it's harder than a steel beam.

"You wanna feel my tonsils, don't you? You want me to gag on it, don't you?" I ask.

"Yes, I wanna feel your mouth all over him. I miss the way your mouth feels on him," Sage replies.

"I know you miss my mesmerizing head, but I can't suck him just yet," I say.

"Sheena, why not? Don't you know once he's hard like that I need to release? You aren't gonna leave me with blue balls are you?" Sage asks.

"No, I don't plan to leave you with blue balls. I wouldn't do that to you. I can't suck him because I need you to do something for me first," I say.

"Oh, I get it. You want to receive before you give. I'm cool with that. Get on the bed and spread your legs and I'll eat you until you cum all over my face," Sage narrates.

I say, "That's music to my ears. We'll get to that, but that's not it. You have "ball breath". Your nuts need to be freshened up. I'm not going down on you until you wash them."

"That's wrong," Sage says jokingly.

I tell Sage that there are washcloths in the linen closet. He goes to the bathroom to freshen up. His balls actually smelled fine, but I needed to get him out of my sight for a moment. While

Sage is in the bathroom, I scurry to my guest bedroom to check on Kevin. He is ready to get the plan moving forward.

I go back to my bedroom after briefly talking to Kevin. I fix Sage and me a shot of tequila. I tell Sage to hurry up because I'm ready to taste his dick. Sage exits the bathroom moments later.

"Is he all freshened up?" I ask.

"So fresh and so clean, clean," Sage says in a singing manner.

"Okay, let's toast," I say as I hand Sage his glass.

"What are we toasting to?" Sage asks.

I reply, "We are toasting to a new beginning and a second chance to make things right."

"I like the sound of that," Sage says as he pulls me close to him.

We both down our shot of Patrón. Sage is half naked, so I feel compelled to get him completely naked. I love seeing a well-built man fully exposed. It does something to me. It's a natural aphrodisiac. I order Sage to get comfortable on the bed while I serve him. He immediately complies.

Sage is stretched across the bed comfortably. I begin licking his chest while I stroke his dick. His dick is not getting hard like it was moments ago. Sage's speech is even beginning to get slow and slurred. I guess the "mickey" I slipped in his drink is working. Two minutes later, Sage is completely unconscious.

I make sure Sage is really out of it and I gather his clothes before I go to get Kevin out of the other room. Kevin is anxiously waiting for me. I give him Sage's clothes for him to put on.

"Are you sure this is really worth it?" Kevin asks.

"Are you scared that he's going to beat your ass again?" I question.

"No, I'm not scared. I'm just saying," Kevin says.

"And I'm just saying you let him whoop your ass and he played with your mind. You can't let him get that. He manipulated you. You know what, I'll just handle it. Get out the damn way," I say.

I know the attack on his ego is too hard on him to not go along with the plan. He may not want to do it, but his pride will make him. He can't let another man get the best of him. Sometimes you have to hit the right buttons to get a man to do what you want. Fortunately, for me, I know exactly what buttons to push to get the men in my life moving.

"I'm good. I'll do it. I don't want to alter the plan. It's entirely his fault that this is happening anyway. Karma's a bitch," Kevin states.

"Yes, it's entirely his fault. Now, hurry up and put his clothes on. Here goes his car keys and phone too. The gas can is in the trunk of Sage's car, but he already put the gas in my car. Unfortunately, you're gonna have to put some more gas in it. Don't forget to keep your face from directly looking into the cameras," I state.

Kevin vocalizes, "I'll take care of it. There's a gas station on the way."

"Okay. I didn't expect him to put the gas in the tank without checking with me first. Oh, but make sure you don't drive his car into the gas station," I instruct.

Kevin states, "Sheena, you need to relax. I'm not a dumb ass. I told you I'll take care of it. You can believe I'll handle it properly."

Kevin leaves my house in Sage's car. Sage is sound asleep in my bed. I hope I didn't give him too much of that stuff that knocked him out. I just want him unconscious for a few hours, but not dead. I can easily tell he's sleeping though.

Kevin follows the plan and drives to In the Mix and parks down the street. He grabs the gas can from out of the trunk and carries it to the club. As part of the plan, I text Kevin on Sage's phone. I ask what he's doing and his response is taking care of some business at the club. I know if it comes down to an investigation, the police will be able to track Sage's cell phone records and it'll look pretty bad for him if his phone records indicate that he was near the club.

The GPS in his car will also show that he drove to the club. I even told Sage I needed gas for my car, so he stopped and filled his fuel jug for me. Kevin begins to pour the gasoline all around the outside of the club. He pours it along the walls of the club and in several different locations.

Kevin finishes dispensing the gasoline from the container and sets it on fire. Next, he hurries back to Sage's car and drives back to my house. He comes upstairs and goes straight into the guest bedroom. He tells me everything went according to plan. I help him out of Sage's clothes and walk him downstairs.

I say, "Thanks for your help. I'll call you tomorrow."

If only he knew that I can't stand him either. I just needed him to get this done. I will only talk to him for the sake of our son once this blows over. I will keep in contact with him for the moment because I don't need him doing something reckless because I'm not speaking to him. I have to keep him under my thumb.

Kevin leaves and I go check on Sage. He is still knocked out cold. I am more than satisfied to know that his place of business is burning down to the ground. His phone begins to ring off the hook and I'm sure it's people calling to tell him his place is burning down.

I decide to take a nice hot bath while I sip more wine. Damn, revenge feels so good. Sage only cares about his dick and his club. I couldn't harm him physically, but I got his club for sure. He attempted to burn my love life and friendship, so I burned down his place of business. It seems like a balanced equation to me.

I wait a little while longer before I attempt to wake Sage up. I go over to the bed and rub his chest and call his name softly. He doesn't respond to anything I'm doing initially. I decide to shake him and call his name louder. He begins to awaken, but is very groggy.

CHAPTER 19
Sheena's Perspective

"You must be working like a slave because you fell out before I could work my magic on you. You had to be exhausted. I don't ever remember you falling asleep on me," I say.

Sage replies, "I just recall getting real tired and weak. I remember you stroking my dick and then it all went dark."

"Well, I hope you slept okay. That was your body sending you a message. We often think everything is all good, but little do we know that things are awry," I say.

If only he knew what I really mean by that statement. He's going to be sick to his stomach in a few minutes. I chat with him for a few more minutes before he fully wakes up. I tell him the reason why I woke him up.

"I normally wouldn't have disturbed you

while sleeping, but your phone has been ringing incessantly for hours. Your text messages were blowing up too. I didn't know if an emergency had arisen," I report.

"What time is it? Where's my phone? How long was I out for?" Sage questions.

I reply, "It's two in the morning and you were out for hours. I put your phone on my nightstand. I hope you don't mind, but I turned it to silent because it kept going off. Maybe it was one or many of your women."

Sage replies, as he goes to retrieve his phone, "Cut it out. You know that isn't my swag anymore. I don't need multiple women to satisfy me. I just need one good one. Miss, I just need you."

As he looks at his messages, I can see him realize what I've known for hours. His jaws drop further down than a sunken ship at the bottom of the ocean.

"Damn it! It is an emergency. The club caught on fire tonight," Sage reports.

"Oh my, are you serious?" I ask.

Sage grabs his clothes and rushes for the door. He is visibly shaken by the news of his beloved club being destroyed. I don't feel sorry for him one bit. I put on my clothes and leave the house to head down to the club. I just want to see how badly the club has been damaged. I'll also get a kick out seeing Sage's face filled with anger and hurt.

To my surprise, Eric is sitting on my porch when I pull out of the garage. What the hell is he doing here? I know he's been calling me all day, but it's the middle of the night and he shouldn't be here. Sage just left, so I'm sure Eric saw him leave. If he saw Sage, he will have an issue with it. I normally wouldn't care, but I was planning to call him tomorrow when everything was settled. I jump out of the car and greet him.

"Hi, Eric. I really didn't expect to see you here at this time of night," I say.

"I bet you didn't. I guess you didn't notice my calls and texts all day either. It really disgusts me how you could be so insensitive to my feelings. I miss the sweet and caring Sheena who I fell in love with. You need to bring her back," Eric states.

"I'm here in front of you. I've not gone anywhere. I was going to call you in the morning, so we could talk and get this worked out. Eric, I've missed you," I say as I reach up to caress his face.

Eric moves his face away and asks, "You've missed me so much that you've avoided me all damn day and all week? Where they do that at?"

I reply, "Trust me. I will call you in the morning and this will be settled tomorrow. I can't talk about this right now. I have somewhere to be. I need to go now."

"You have your ex-boyfriend leaving here in the middle of the night after you've disregarded me all day, but you say I should trust you. That's funny as hell. Sheena, you are something else," Eric observes.

"I know what it looks like, but it's not what you think. I promise," I assert.

"If you are sincere and truthful in what you're saying, then stay here with me and we can talk now. We don't have to wait until tomorrow," Eric narrates.

"I'm sorry Eric, but that is impossible right now. You'll just have to wait until tomorrow," I declare.

When I tell Eric that I'm leaving, he becomes extremely agitated. He clearly thinks that I have rekindled my relationship with Sage, but he is wrong. The only thing being kindled right now is In the Mix and I want to see it. Burn baby burn. I get back into my car, so I can leave.

"Fuck you Sheena. That's all I can say, is fuck you. If you wanna chase Sage after the way he treated you, it's fine with me. You can have him because I'm finished with you. You really are too immature for me anyway," Eric claims.

I say, "Bitch bye."

I wave my hand at Eric and pull off. Hell, I have more important things to deal with than his sensitive ass. I call Rachel and Ilesha to tell them to meet me at In the Mix, so they can share in this moment with me. I know Sage didn't care about my feelings when he set Kevin up to think he slept with Ilesha, so I damn sure don't care about his feelings. The girls get to the scene shortly after I do.

There are a lot of people gathered out here. Many of the people gathered are patrons of the club, others are fire fighters and other investigators. The building is still smoldering and has suffered significant damage. Sage is livid and confused. He can't figure out how this happened. I want to tell him right now, but I'll wait.

Me and my girls have a devilish grin on our faces every time we make eye contact. I'm trying not to burst out laughing. I walk over to Sage and rub his back and let him know that everything will be okay. He doesn't seem to be moved by my insincere comment.

I can't help but think about how much damage has been done. The exterior is burnt very badly and the roof has caved in. I'm sure the inside is a total loss too. Whatever isn't damaged from the fire is definitely ruined from the water damage.

This is the moment I lived for ever since I found out that Sage is the one who plotted against me. He is walking up to every fire fighter he sees trying to get answers to his many questions. Hopefully, he feels the same stress I felt when Kevin told me he fucked one of my friends. He can't stand still. He seems to have aged ten years in ten minutes.

Sage summons me over to him. I'm glad he does because I want an up close and personal view of every twitch of his facial expressions and body movement. Sage and I walk with the fire chief to the side of the building. The fire chief tells Sage what caused the fire.

The fire chief says, "This is definitely a case of arson sir."

Sage is flabbergasted by the fire chief's response. I decide to play along and act surprised. Sage has a very confused look on his face.

"Arson? Are you sure sir?" Sage asks.

The fire chief replies, "I've been doing this probably since before you were born young man. I'm very sure that someone deliberately caused this fire."

The fire chief shows us where he feels the fire started. He also tells us that an accelerant was used to start the blaze. I know it was no accident. Sage is devastated. You can tell he doesn't know what to do or how to respond.

Sage replies, "I understand sir. I wasn't challenging your expertise. It's just that it is extremely hard to take all of this in. I've spent a long time trying to build this place up."

"It's okay. I understand this is a great loss for you, but at least nobody was hurt and only your establishment suffered damage. It could have been a lot worse," says the fire chief.

"Thank you, sir. I appreciate all of your help," Sage replies.

The fire department has cleared the building

and told Sage that he can enter the premises. We go inside the club and it's decimated. I don't know what caused more damage to the club. The fire took a toll, but so did the fire fighters. Sage goes into what used to be his office. It's also in pretty bad shape.

Sage states, "I still can't believe that someone would burn my club down. I hope the surveillance cameras are able to identify the perpetrator. His ass is going down!"

"Yeah, hopefully so. You know you are on top of your security. The cameras will definitely show something damning," I say.

"I'm sure I'll get something. Even if my machines are damaged, it won't matter because all of the video surveillance is backed up to a remote server," Sage reports.

"Good, because you really need to get to the bottom of this. The answer may be right in front of you," I say.

I could not resist throwing that comment at him. I know he's going to want to snap my neck when he finds out that I'm responsible for this. I'll make sure we aren't alone when I break the news to him. Unfortunately, the cameras in here are so badly damaged that Sage can't retrieve his video footage.

I need to see his face when he watches the video surveillance of the person setting his place on fire. If he thinks he's confused and angry now, wait until he sees what looks like him committing arson against his own business. Sage mentions calling his insurance company to start the process of getting things taken care of, but I tell him to wait.

"Sage, it's the middle of the night. Those insurance people aren't in the office yet. You aren't thinking clearly. The best bet is to go see the video if you can," I offer.

"Yeah, you're right. My mind is blown. The footage is backed up at my house, so I need to go home. There's nothing left to do here," Sage replies.

I want Rachel and Ilesha to provide protection just in case Sage flips out on me. I tell Sage to give me his car keys and I can have Rachel or Ilesha drive my car. Sage questions why I want his keys. I tell him that he's in no shape to drive and it may be best if I take him home.

I really just need to have an excuse for my girls to be by my side when he sees the video. Of course, he falls for my bullshit reason and turns over his keys.

"I'm gonna go talk to Rachel and Ilesha for a moment. I'll be outside when you're ready to go," I recite.

"Okay, I'll be out soon," Sage says.

"Take your time. I'm here for you," I comment.

I really am here for him, but not how he thinks. I walk outside and talk to my girls.

"Damn, you really fucked this place up. I don't even recognize it anymore," notes Ilesha.

Rachel mentions, "You really brought the whole building down. Maybe you could have yelled at him very loudly to get your point across. I know he's hurting inside."

"Rachel, you can miss me with all of the talking. Sage doesn't care about words. Besides, he tried to break up our sisterhood and nobody does that. He waged war against us and had to pay expensively," I explain.

Rachel states, "I guess."

Ilesha replies, "Ain't no guessing. His ass got what he deserved. We didn't bother him. He came for us and lost."

I let them know that they'll be following us to Sage's place. Moments later, Sage comes out of the smoldering rubble and motions with a hand signal that he's ready to go. Ilesha and Rachel both wave at him as they head to the car. I walk over to Sage and we head to his car.

Rachel and Ilesha are pulling up behind me and Sage by the time we make it to the car. They follow us to Sage's house. The entire way to Sage's house he talks about how angry he is about all of this.

"The person responsible for this is going to pay. I'll see that they spend a lot of time in jail behind this. I have plenty of connections in D.C.," Sage comments.

I totally agree with him because he is the one

who is responsible for all of this and he is paying for it. He's paying for it emotionally and will be paying for it financially. We arrive at Sage's place and it's beautiful. I have never been here before. I thought his last home was beautiful, but it has nothing on this one. Even my girls are in awe of his mini mansion.

We head inside and Sage wastes no time going for the footage. He doesn't even offer to show us around the house. We aren't getting a tour or a drink. I don't care because I just need to see one thing and that's his face when he sees the video.

Sage goes to his computer and pulls up the footage of the fire. He sees an individual walking up to the club carrying a red gas jug. He watches every move the man makes like a vulture does when stalking its prey. Sage isn't saying a word. He's totally locked in. I look over my shoulder at the girls and they smirk at me.

Sage speaks, "Come on bastard. Let the camera see your face. Let me see your face."

The person dumps the gas and ignites the fire and is eventually off the camera and out of sight. Sage is livid because he didn't get the person's identity from the footage. He is just standing here cursing up a storm and shaking his head. If he could see my insides right now, he'd be able to see that I'm filled with satisfaction. This feeling is like a prolonged orgasm and I don't want it to stop. I love it!

"Sage, I know this may not be the right time for you to discuss this because of how you feel right now, but I think it is," I impart.

"I really don't want to talk about my feelings right now. I have to focus on getting to the bottom of this," Sage replies.

"Well, this will help you get to the bottom of this and this conversation isn't about your feelings, it's pertaining to your damn club," I say.

"Please enlighten me," Sage replies.

"You sent your little waitress bitch to fuck my man and make it look like Ilesha did it. That's the lowest shit anybody ever did to me. Even lower than what you did to me before. You know my girls are my sisters and you sought to tear us apart," I utter.

Ilesha expresses, "That was some real fucked up shit. I normally cut people for bullshit like that, but Sheena stopped me for some reason."

"Please don't try to deny it. We know the entire story. You'll only look worse," says Rachel.

Sage pauses for a moment as if to collect his thoughts. He is very careful about the things he says and does, so him pausing isn't surprising. We wait patiently for his response and the room is in dead silence.

"Alright, I sent my waitress to your man's house, but don't blame me for him cheating because he wanted it. He was eyeing Ilesha all night and even came to talk to me about her. I saw an opening, so I took it. I didn't make him fuck her," Sage narrates.

I insist, "You are just like you were when we were together. Always scheming and manipulating people. It never stops with you. I can't keep doing this with you. I can't."

"Talk about the pot calling the kettle black. It seems that you are quite the master manipulator yourself. Don't forget that you had two boyfriends not too long ago. It looks like you and I are very much alike," Sage shoots back.

"Okay, it all makes sense now. That entire charade is about you being jealous of me and what I'm doing," I say.

Ilesha states, "He's the typical man. Doesn't want to do right by you when you're together, but the moment you move on, here they come with their bullshit."

Rachel vocalizes, "It's so true. I've seen this too many times. It makes me cry at night. The injustices of man."

Sage replies, "Sheena, you need to accept the blame for why all of this happened. It's really your fault. I'm just being honest."

"I have to hear this. I can't believe that you are going to try to make this my fault. Let's hear it," I say.

Sage states, "You played a game on me, so I felt it necessary to retaliate against you."

"Cut it out Sage. I've played no games with you. Stop it. This is a poor attempt to not man up and take ownership for your actions," I respond.

"Let's talk about the night before the Halloween party when I was eating you out. You stopped me and told me I was tasting Kevin's and Eric's dicks. I know you didn't think I was gonna let that slide. That was a dirty game you played, so I played mine," says Sage.

"You thought to break up my relationships and friendship over that? That was between you and me. You coulda cursed me out or threw me out of the club. You went too far," I say.

"That's a matter of opinion. What's too far of a reaction for one person, is perfectly normal to another person," Sage states.

We all go back and forth arguing and we are getting nothing out of this. There is nothing left to say, so me and the girls decide it's time to leave. The longer we stay increases the chances of something sideways happening. Ilesha will really cut Sage and think nothing about it.

"We are out of here," I disclose.

"Hell no you aren't! You said this conversation would help me get to the bottom of the arson situation. I need some clarity on that before you leave," communicates Sage.

"Look back at the video. The person is about your height and is dressed in your clothes. It really looks like you set your own place on fire for the insurance money," I remark.

"Nobody would ever believe that. That's bullshit and you know it. I was with you all

225

night!" Sage screams.

"I don't know about that Sage. Maybe you were and maybe you weren't, but it really looks quite bad for you. This is your payback for fucking with me and my girls. I'm not one of those lil girls in the streets you play with. I'm all woman," I explain.

Sage conveys, "You have lost your mind. I know you aren't trying to make this look like I did it."

"Well, let's consider a few things. One, the guy is wearing the same clothes you have on right now. Two, I'm your only alibi. Three, you bought gas before you came to my house. The list goes on, but just know if you file an insurance claim, I'll bury you. Insurance fraud and arson are felonies. I'm sure you don't want me to make an anonymous call to the authorities," I narrate.

Rachel phrases, "This reminds me of that Lauren Hill song. You know, the one called 'Lost Ones'. That is so symbolic of now."

"She definitely dropped a bomb on him," Ilesha jokes.

"Calm down ladies. Calm down. The celebration is over. That call to authorities will not be needed and also will not be in the best interest of any of us. That's simply not an option here," states Sage.

"Girls, we are all done here. This one's over," I say.

"We aren't done here. Since we're in the

mood for dropping bombs, I have one to drop on you before you go," professes Sage.

Sage goes over to his safe and grabs an envelope with the logo of the clinic where I got my paternity tests performed. As he walks closer, he has a devilish smirk on his face. He hands me the envelope and it has my name on it. I can't imagine why Sage would have anything from the clinic with my name on it. I open the envelope immediately and examine the contents of it.

"Sage, what the fuck? You can't be serious!" I scream.

EPILOGUE

Ladies, I know that burning down Sage's club was against the law, but it had to be done. Men only respect strength. If we show any sign of weakness, they will pounce on us and go for the jugular. You have to be willing to do the unthinkable sometimes to make them comprehend the severity of the situation. The best way to make a man understand how we feel is to force him into the exact same situation. Ladies, you can't just tell them you're mad or hurt; you have to make men feel the identical emotion you're feeling.

I could have put sugar in his gas tank or bust the windows out of his car, but we've seen that too many times. Doing that may shock them for a moment, but it doesn't set them back. I wanted to set Sage back. I wanted his hurt to be ten times worse than my discomfort. I knew Sage's weak spot was his precious club, so I took it away from him and there's nothing he can do about it. Every day his club is closed is bad for him. He's losing money every second In the Mix is not open. If a man gets out of line, you have to stick it to him and let him know that you're in control. It's our world ladies and we need to proceed as such.